## "Gray, I'm scared."

"You'd be an idiot not to be scared." He surprised her, both with the low fervency of his words and by what he did next.

He dropped his head forward so his brow rested on hers. She'd never before thought of him as a man who needed to lean, but in that moment, she felt as though they were propping each other up.

"Gray?" she said, the single word a question that encompassed all the thoughts inside her head. *What's going on?* she wanted to ask, *Do you feel it, too?* But she didn't have the guts.

"I'll protect you," he said. The three words of the heartfelt vow, punched through her because she instinctively knew he wasn't just promising to protect a witness. He was promising to protect *her.*

"I know you will," she said, trying not to make more of this than it really was. "Because it's your job."

"And because of this," he replied. Then he tipped her face up, and touched his lips to hers.

# JESSICA ANDERSEN

# MOUNTAIN INVESTIGATION

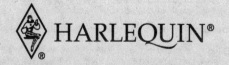

HARLEQUIN®

TORONTO • NEW YORK • LONDON
AMSTERDAM • PARIS • SYDNEY • HAMBURG
STOCKHOLM • ATHENS • TOKYO • MILAN • MADRID
PRAGUE • WARSAW • BUDAPEST • AUCKLAND

Recycling programs
for this product may
not exist in your area.

ISBN-13: 978-0-373-69414-3

MOUNTAIN INVESTIGATION

## ABOUT THE AUTHOR

Though she's tried out professions ranging from cleaning sea lion cages to cloning glaucoma genes, from patent law to training horses, Jessica is happiest when she's combining all these interests with her first love: writing romances. These days she's delighted to be writing full-time on a farm in rural Connecticut that she shares with a small menagerie and a hero named Brian. She hopes you'll visit her at www.JessicaAndersen.com for info on upcoming books, contests and to say "hi!"

## Books by Jessica Andersen

HARLEQUIN INTRIGUE
734—DR. BODYGUARD
762—SECRET WITNESS
793—INTENSIVE CARE
817—BODY SEARCH
833—COVERT M.D.
850—THE SHERIFF'S DAUGHTER
868—BULLSEYE
893—RICOCHET*
911—AT CLOSE RANGE*
928—RAPID FIRE*
945—RED ALERT
964—UNDER THE MICROSCOPE
982—PRESCRIPTION: MAKEOVER
1005—CLASSIFIED BABY
1012—MEET ME AT MIDNIGHT
1036—DOCTOR'S ORDERS
1061—TWIN TARGETS
1068—WITH THE M.D....AT THE ALTAR?
1093—MANHUNT IN THE WILD WEST*
1120—SNOWED IN WITH THE BOSS
1147—MOUNTAIN INVESTIGATION*

*Bear Claw Creek Crime Lab

# CAST OF CHARACTERS

*Mariah Shore*—The ex-wife of escaped convict Lee Mawadi lives in fear that he'll return to carry out his threats, but experience has taught her not to trust members of law enforcement—especially not one like sexy FBI agent Michael Grayson.

*Michael (Gray) Grayson*—This revenge-driven agent will stop at nothing to avenge the deaths of the ones he loved... even if it means endangering a woman whose only crime was falling for the wrong man.

*Lee Mawadi*—An American by birth, a terrorist by inclination and indoctrination, Lee needs Mariah's help in the next stage of a terrorist plot...then he'll kill her for daring to divorce him.

*Al-Jihad*—The terrorist leader has a far-reaching network and a multilevel terror plan involving Bear Claw Creek.

*SAC Johnson*—Gray's boss doesn't like or trust him...maybe for good reason.

*Jonah Fairfax*—Gray's only true ally understands what it feels like for an agent to be torn between love and duty.

*Brisbane (aka Felix Smith)*—Is the too-big thug Mariah's ally...or her greatest enemy?

# Chapter One

Mariah Shore paused on the ridgeline about a half mile from her isolated cabin. Standing in the lee of a sturdy pine, she scanned the woods around her with a photographer's sharp eye. She wasn't looking for a subject for her old, beloved Canon 35 mm, though. The camera was stowed safely in her backpack for the hike home.

No, she was looking for a target for the Remington double-aught shotgun she held across her body.

"There's nobody there," she told herself, willing it to be true. But the woods were quieter than she liked, and the day was rapidly dimming toward the too-early springtime dusk.

With her curvy figure swathed in lined pants, a flannel shirt, a wool sweater and a down parka, and her dark curls tucked under a thick knit cap, she'd be warm enough if she stayed put. But her hurry to get home wasn't about the warmth. It was about the cabin's thick walls and sturdy locks, the line of electric fencing near the trees, and the motion-sensitive lights and alarms that formed a protective perimeter around the clear-cut yard.

The cabin was safe. Outside was a crapshoot.

She needed to keep moving, would've been nearly home if she hadn't heard a crackle of underbrush and seen a flash of movement directly in her path. She'd tried to tell herself it was just an animal, but she'd spent the best weeks of her childhood following her grandfather through Colorado woods like these, and she'd lived in the cabin thirty miles north of Bear Claw City for more than a year now. She'd hiked out nearly every day since arriving, first for peace and more recently for some actual work, as she'd started to feel the stirrings of the creativity she'd thought was gone for good. She knew the forest, knew the rhythms and inhabitants of the ridgeline. Whatever was between her and the cabin, her sense of the woods told her it wasn't a bear or wildcat. Her gut said it was two-legged danger.

Her ex-husband. Lee Mawadi.

Or was it?

"He's not there," she told herself. "He's long gone."

She'd kept tabs on the investigation, listening to the infrequent follow-ups on her small radio, and asking careful questions during her rare trips into the city for supplies. Because of that, she knew there had been no sign of Lee in the nearly six months since he and three other men had escaped from the ARX Supermax Prison, located on the other side of the ridge. She also knew—or logic dictated, anyway—that her ex-husband had no real reason to come back to the area, and every reason to stay away.

After a long moment, when nothing could be heard but the muted sounds of the sun-loving animals powering down and the nocturnal creatures revving up as dusk fell along the ridgeline, she even managed to believe her own words.

"You're talking yourself into being scared," she muttered, slinging the double-aught over her shoulder and heading for home. "There's no way he's coming back here."

Lee might be a terrorist, a murderer and a liar, but he wasn't stupid.

Still, she stayed alert as she walked, relaxing only slightly when it seemed like the forest noises got a little louder, as though whatever menace the woodland creatures had sensed—if anything—had passed through and gone.

When Mariah reached the fifty-foot perimeter around the cabin, the motion-sensitive lights snapped on. The bright illumination showed a wide swath of stumps in stark relief, mute evidence of the terror that had driven her to chainsaw every tree within a fifty-foot radius of the cabin, and install a low-lying, solar-powered electric fence to keep the animals away.

In the center of the clear-cut zone sat the cabin. It was sturdy and thick-walled, its proportions slightly off, a bit top-heavy, and if she'd thought a time or two that she and the cabin were very much alike, there was nobody around to agree or disagree with her. She lived alone, and was grateful for the solitude. She used to think she wanted the hustle and bustle of a city, and the mob of friends she'd lacked during childhood. Now she knew better. Once a loner, always a loner.

Reaching into her pocket for the small remote control she carried with her at all times, she deactivated the motion-sensitive alarms. The security system wasn't wired to call for any sort of outside response, first because she was too far off the beaten track for the police to do her any good, and second because she didn't have much use for cops. That wasn't why she'd installed the system; she'd wanted it as a warning, pure and simple. If she was in the cabin and trouble appeared, she'd know it was time to get out—or dig in and defend herself. If she was somewhere in the forest, she'd have a head start on escaping.

The Bear Claw cops and the Feds had offered her protection, of course, first when Lee had been arrested for his terrorist activities, and again when he'd escaped. But those offers had all come with questions and sidelong looks, and the threat of people in her space, watching her every move, making it clear that she was as much a suspect as a victim.

*Victim.* Oh, how she hated the word, hated knowing she'd been one. Not as much a victim as the people Lee had killed, or the families who mourned the dead, but a victim nonetheless. Worse, she'd been selfish and blind, not looking beyond the problems in her marriage to see the larger threat. She had to live with that, would do so until the day she died. But that didn't mean she had to live with strangers—worse, cops and FBI agents—reminding her of it, and hounding her and her parents. Not when there wasn't anything she could do to help them find her ex-husband.

"There's no way he's coming back here," she repeated, shifting the shotgun farther back on her shoulder so she could fumble in her pocket for the keys to the log cabin's front door. "He'd be an idiot to even try."

She unlocked the door and pushed through into the cabin, starting to relax as she keyed the remote to bring the motion-sensitive alarms back online.

They shrieked, warning that something—or some-*one*— had breached the perimeter in the short moment the alarms had been off.

A split second later, a blur came at her from the side and a heavy hand clamped on her arm, bringing a sharp pricking pain. Jolting, Mariah screamed and spun, but the spin turned into a sideways lurch as her legs went watery and her muscles gave out.

*Drugs,* she thought, realizing that a syringe had been the source of the prick, drugs the source of the spinning disconnection that seized her, dampening her ability to fight or flee. The tranquilizer didn't blunt her panic, though, or the sick knowledge that she was in serious trouble. Her heart hammered and her soul screamed, *No!*

She fell, and a man grabbed her on the way down, his fingers digging into the flesh of her upper arms. His face was blurred by whatever he'd given her, but she knew it was Lee. She recognized the shape of her ex's body, the pain of his hard grasp and the way her skin crawled beneath his touch.

He took the remote control from her, and used it to kill the alarm. Then he leaned in close, and his features became sharp and familiar: close-cropped, white-blond hair; smooth, elegant skin; and blue eyes that could go from friendly to murderous in a snap.

Born to an upper-class Boston family, the second son of loving parents with a strong marriage, Lee Chisholm had been sent to the best schools and given all the opportunities a child could've asked for. Logic said he should have matured into the cultured, successful man he'd looked like when Mariah had met him. And on one level, he'd been that man. On another, he'd been a spoiled monster whose parents had hidden the fact that he'd had a taste for arson and violence. That nasty child had grown into a man in search of a cause, an excuse to indulge his evil appetites. He'd found that cause during his years at an exclusive, expensive college, where he'd been recruited into the anti-American crusade.

As part of a terrorist cell, under the leadership of mastermind al-Jihad, he'd gone by the name of Lee Mawadi, and had arranged to meet Mariah because of her father's connections to one of al-Jihad's targets. Lee had wooed her, courted her, pretended to love her…and then he'd used her and set her up to die.

She hadn't died, but in the years since, she hadn't really lived, either. And now, seeing her own death in her ex-husband's face, she cringed from him, her heart hammering against her ribs, tears leaking from her eyes.

*Lee, no. Don't!* she tried to say, but the words didn't come, and the scream stayed locked in her throat because she couldn't move, couldn't struggle, couldn't do anything other than hang limply in his grasp and suck in a thin trickle of air.

Then he let go of her. She fell to the floor at the threshold of the cabin and landed hard, winding up in a tangled heap of arms and legs, lax muscles and terror.

He crouched over her, gloating as he held up the

small styrette he'd used to drug her. "This is to shut you up and keep you where you belong," he said. Then he stood, drew back his foot and kicked her in the stomach. Pain sang through her, radiating from the soft place where the blow landed. She would've curled around the agony, but she couldn't do even that. She could only lie there, tears running down her face as he said, "That was for forgetting where you belong, *wife*. Which is by my side, no matter what."

He grabbed her by the hood of her parka and dragged her inside, kicking the door shut.

The sound of it closing was a death knell, because Mariah knew one thing for certain: the man she'd once promised to love, honor and obey didn't intend to let her leave the cabin alive.

*Five days later*

Michael Grayson was a man on a mission, and he didn't intend to let inconsequential details like due process or official sanction interfere. Which was why, just shy of six months after he'd nearly been booted out of the FBI for sidestepping protocol, Gray was back on the edge of the line between agent and renegade, between law officer and vigilante. Only this time he was well aware of it and knew the consequences; his superiors had put him on notice, loud and clear.

The threats didn't stop him from taking his day off to drive up through the heart of Bear Claw Canyon State Forest to the hills beyond, though, and they didn't keep him from using a pair of bolt cutters on the padlocked gate that barred entry to a narrow access road leading up the ridgeline. Up to *her* house.

He drove into the forest as far as he dared, just past a fire access road that marked the two-thirds point of the journey. He tucked his four-by-four into the trees, off the main track so it couldn't be seen easily from the road, pointing it downhill in the event that he needed to get out of there fast.

Then he started walking, staying off the main road and out of sight, just in case. As he did so, he tried to tell himself that it was recon, nothing more, that he just wanted to get a look at Lee Mawadi's ex-wife six months after the prison break. But he couldn't make the lie play, even inside his own skull. His gut said that Mariah Shore had secrets. There had to be a reason she'd moved into a cabin on a ridgeline that, on a clear day, provided views of both Bear Claw City and the ARX Supermax Prison.

His coworkers and superiors in the Denver field office had put zero stock in Gray's gut feelings—which admittedly had a bit of a hit-or-miss reputation. The higher-ups had written Mariah off as nothing more than she seemed: a pretty, dark-haired woman who'd married a man in good faith, not realizing that he was using her twice over, once to create the illusion of middle-American normalcy and disguise his ties to al-Jihad's terrorist network, and a second time to gain entrée to her family.

When the newlyweds moved to a suburb north of Bear Claw City to be close to her parents, Mariah had leaned on her father to find a job for her engineering-trained husband within the American Mall Group, where her father had been an upper-level manager. It wasn't until after the attacks and subsequent arrests, when the story had started coming together, that it became clear Lee had manipulated Mariah into getting him the job, just as he'd manipulated her into serving as his alibi through the first few rounds of the investigation.

Or so she had claimed. Gray hadn't fully bought her protestations of innocence two years earlier during the original investigation, and he sure as hell hadn't believed them more recently, when her husband had escaped. There were only so many times he could hear "I don't know anything" before it started to wear thin, especially when the suspect's actions said otherwise.

Mariah Chisholm, who had gone back to using her maiden name of Shore after the divorce, knew more than she was admitting. Gray was positive of it…he just couldn't convince his jackass, rules-are-God boss, Special Agent in Charge Johnson, to lean on her harder.

Then again, SAC Johnson was in this investigation to make his career and avoid stepping on any political toes. Gray was in it for justice.

The horrific terror attacks two and a half years earlier, dubbed the "Santa Bombings," had targeted the start of the holiday season, when families with young children had gathered at each of the American Malls to welcome the mall Santas. The bombs had been concealed in building stress points near the elaborate thrones where the Santas had sat for whispered consultations with hundreds of hopeful, holiday-crazed kids. The explosives had all gone off simultaneously, in six malls across the state. Hundreds had been killed—families destroyed in a flash—during the most joyous of seasons.

It had been an inhuman attack, directed solely at the most innocent of innocents. Terrorism in the truest sense of the word.

In the investigation immediately afterwards, a couple of sales receipts and a glitchy security camera had led the FBI agents to Lee Chisholm—who called himself Mawadi among his "real" family within the terror network—along with his co-conspirator, Muhammad Feyd, and the mastermind himself, al-Jihad. The evidence had been enough to convict the men—barely—and get them sentenced to life-plus at the ARX Supermax. The clues hadn't seemed to point to the involvement of Mawadi's wife, who at the time had been dealing with bad press, a quickie divorce and her father's forced retirement and subsequent near-fatal heart attack. In the end, Mariah Chisholm, née Shore, had been cleared of suspicion as far as the higher-ups were concerned.

As far as Gray was concerned, though, they'd missed something.

He'd been part of the initial interviews of Mariah and her father, and he'd memorized all the reports—both the official file and the assembled news stories. The reports from two years earlier, during the time when Lee Mawadi had been arrested, tried and convicted, had described Mariah as "shocked," "devastated" and "grief-stricken." One Shakespeare of a journalist had even called her a "doe-eyed innocent played false by the man she thought she knew."

The pictures and film clips had backed up those descriptions, showing a lovely, sad-eyed woman with curly, dark-brown hair and full lips that had trembled at all the right moments. For the most part she'd tried to avoid the cameras. On the few occasions she'd spoken publicly, she'd read prepared statements in which she had apologized for not having seen her husband of six months for what he'd been—a monster—and had urged swift justice for Mawadi, Feyd and al-Jihad. Even Gray, an admitted cynic, had bought the routine, all but forgetting about her once Mawadi and the others were behind bars. He'd shifted his attention away from them and focused on tracking down more of al-Jihad's terror cells.

All that had changed the previous fall, though, when Mawadi, Feyd and al-Jihad had escaped from the ARX Supermax with the help of fellow prisoner Jonah Fairfax. Fairfax had proven to be a deep undercover Fed who'd been charged with flushing out al-Jihad's contacts within U.S. law enforcement, and had planned to do so by facilitating the escape and then netting all the conspirators when they made their move. But the setup had backfired badly when it turned out that Fairfax's superior, who had progressively isolated him over the previous two years, had turned, becoming one of al-Jihad's assets.

In the end, Fairfax had helped al-Jihad escape, and the only conspirator he'd flushed out was his own boss, code-named Jane Doe, who had vanished in the aftermath of a foiled attack on a local stadium. The Feds and local cops had managed to recapture Muhammad Feyd, but so far he had refused to talk, which left the authorities pretty much chasing their own tails.

Worse, in the immediate aftermath of the thwarted stadium attack, Gray himself had wound up as a suspect in the conspiracy. Which was just plain stupid.

Yes, he'd failed to pass along a potentially crucial message, but that wasn't because he'd been working for al-Jihad. He'd made the decision in a split second of distraction, a moment when his version of justice and the law had clashed and he'd gotten caught up in his own head, stuck in memories. And yeah, maybe there'd been other factors, too, but they were nothing he couldn't handle. He could—and would—bring the bastards down. No way he was letting the Santa Bombers go free. Not now, not ever. Not after what they'd done.

The thought brought a flash of memory, of concussion and screams, and the rapid flutter of a dying child's chest in the sterile confines of an ICU.

Shaking off the image, Gray forced his mind to focus on the task at hand. Moving silently he worked his way through the thick forest, headed for Mariah Shore's cabin. He had no orders, no official sanction. Hell, he was on probation. He was supposed to be riding a desk, monitoring transcribed chatter and helping with the tip lines.

"I'm just out for a hike," he murmured, keeping his voice very low, even though he hadn't seen or heard anything to indicate that he had company. "Is it my fault I just happened to wander out of the state park and stumble on her cabin?"

It wasn't much as plausible deniability went, but he

was done with waiting around for a break that wasn't coming. He'd helped jail Lee Mawadi, Muhammad Feyd and al-Jihad in the first place, using slightly less than orthodox methods in his zeal to gain some measure of justice for the victims of the Santa Bombings. He'd do the same thing again, even if it meant the end of his career.

"Well, well. Will you look at that?" he said, whistling quietly under his breath as the ex-wife's isolated cabin came into view. He stopped amid the cover of a thick stand of trees and scrubby underbrush, and peered through, scoping out the scene.

It looked like Mariah had been doing some landscaping.

Originally, the cabin had been tucked into the woods, with trees very near the structure, shielding it even from satellite view. Now there was a clear-cut swath a good fifty feet in all directions, with raw stumps giving mute testimony to where trees had once stood. In one corner of the lot, a huge pile of cut and split logs sat beside a gas-powered wood splitter. A thin wisp of smoke rose from the cabin's central chimney, indicating that someone was home, as did the vehicles parked in the side yard. One was the banged-up Jeep Mariah had registered in her name. The other was unfamiliar, a nondescript, dark-blue four-by-four SUV.

*Two cars. Two people, maybe more?* Gray thought, tensing further as a quiver of instinct ran through him.

When he'd asked Mariah Shore point-blank why she'd bought the forest-locked cabin no more than thirty miles from the ARX Supermax Prison, she'd claimed it was a sort of penance. She'd said she wanted to be able to see the prison on one side of her, the city of Bear Claw on the other, that she wanted to be reminded of how many lives had been destroyed because she hadn't recognized her husband for what he was.

And maybe that explanation would've worked for him if she'd come off as the grief-stricken victim she'd played two years earlier. But the newer reports—some of which Gray had written himself—described her as "closed off," "detached," "unfriendly," and "nervous"...which weren't the kind of words he typically associated with innocence. They were more in line with the behavior of a woman who had something to hide.

Unfortunately—as far as Gray was concerned, anyway—a detailed check of her activities since Mawadi's incarceration hadn't turned up any indication that she was in contact with her ex. Heck, she'd kept almost entirely to herself, not even visiting her parents when her father had been hospitalized again a few months ago for his recurring heart problems.

In the absence of evidence to the contrary, and with all the available information suggesting that Mawadi, al-Jihad and Jane Doe had fled the country, SAC Johnson had ended all surveillance of Mariah Shore, despite Gray's protests that she was one of their few remaining local links to the terrorists.

In retrospect, Gray knew he probably should've kept his mouth shut. Rather than making his boss take a second look at the decision, his opinion had only made Johnson dig in harder, to the point that he'd ordered Gray to stay the hell away from Mawadi's ex-wife. But

Johnson hadn't known that she had clear-cut the area around her cabin and strung up what looked to be some serious motion-activated lights and alarms, along with a low electric fence that was no doubt intended to keep deer and other critters out of the monitored zone, lest they trigger the alarms.

She'd turned the place into a fortress.

Question was, why?

"And won't Johnson be glad I just happened to be hiking this way?" Gray murmured, having taken up the dubious habit of talking to himself over the last few years, ever since he and Stacy had split up.

Refusing to think of his ex-wife, or how things had gone so wrong so fast after their so-called "trial" separation just before the bombings, Gray moved out of the concealing brush and eased closer to the cabin, his senses on the highest alert.

He hadn't gone more than two paces before the door swung open, and Lee Mawadi himself stepped out onto the rustic porch. Gray froze, adrenaline shooting through him alongside a surge of vindication and the hard, hot jolt of knowing he'd been right all along.

Mariah Shore was in this conspiracy right up to her pretty little neck.

## Chapter Two

Gray stayed very still. He was wearing camouflage and stood hidden behind a screening layer of trees and underbrush; as long as he didn't move, Mawadi shouldn't be able to see him. Gray wasn't totally motionless, though: his blood raced through his veins and his heart pumped furiously, beating in his ears on a rhythm that said he was right, the ex-wife was part of it, after all.

And Lee Mawadi had very definitely *not* fled the country, as all the reports had indicated.

The bastard stood there—blond and Nordic, loose-limbed and relaxed, cradling a Remington shotgun in the crook of one arm as he scanned the forest. Then he headed for the corner of the porch, shouldered the shotgun, unzipped and urinated, all the while scanning the forest. He seemed to be looking for something, but what? Had he seen Gray skulking in the trees? Was he expecting company?

Mawadi finished and rezipped, then turned toward the still-open door, calling, "You said they'd be here at five, right?"

Gray didn't hear the answer, couldn't tell if the responding voice belonged to a man or a woman. His brain raced, trying to parse the tiny nugget of information. It was just past four o'clock, which meant the meeting was an hour away. And if he could figure out who was coming for the meeting, it could be a huge break in the case, allowing them to identify more of the terrorists, maybe even the traitors they suspected might be working within the Bear Claw Police Department, and maybe even the FBI itself. For half a second, excitement zinged through him at the thought of al-Jihad himself showing up. Gray would give anything to be the one to subdue all of them, the terrorists and the ex-wife, and put them where they belonged—in the ARX Supermax or a grave, either way was fine with him.

Then Gray cursed, realizing that if the newcomers were driving up the mountain, he could be in serious trouble. The only way up the ridgeline to the cabin was the narrow track he'd come up, or the fire-access road that merged with the track just below where he'd parked. His four-by-four was off the road and somewhat hidden, but the concealment was far from foolproof. A driver coming up the lane might see the vehicle, even in the gathering dusk.

Which meant he had two choices. One, he could retrace his path, pronto, in hopes of making it down the ridge and hiding the truck before the other vehicle turned up the road. Then he could boogie down the mountain, get into cell range and call for backup. Or two, he could stay put and hope his four-by-four escaped detection while he cobbled together some sort of a plan to subdue Mawadi and whoever else was in the cabin, then capture the others when they arrived.

Gray wasn't a glory seeker by a long shot, but for both personal and professional reasons, he liked the image of dragging in the murdering bastards himself. Not to mention that there was a good chance that even if he made it to cell range, SAC Johnson and the others would give him a less than enthusiastic response. Gray had cried "wolf" before and it had come to nothing, and then he'd dropped the ball on that damn message during the festival, with the result that al-Jihad and the others had very nearly succeeded in their aim of destroying a stadium filled with tens of thousands of city residents awaiting a benefit concert. Which meant that Gray wasn't exactly the go-to guy for anything these days. For all he knew, Johnson would ignore his report and put him back on administrative leave for going near the cabin in the first place.

*All of which is one big, fat rationalization,* Gray admitted inwardly, staying quiet because Mawadi was still on the porch. But spoken aloud or not, it was the truth. He was making up excuses for doing what he fully intended to do, whether or not it was reasonable. He was going in now and alone, not just because he didn't trust Johnson and the other special agents in the Denver office, but because he didn't trust the system itself. Not anymore.

The system hadn't stopped pampered rich-boy Lee Chisholm from taking his love of violence and his knee-jerk hatred of his father's politics and turning it into terrorism. The system hadn't been able to pin any one of a half-dozen other crimes on al-Jihad in the years between the 9/11 terror attacks and the Santa Bombings. The system had let down all the men, women and children who'd died in the attacks; it had failed them and their families twice over—once by not preventing the bombings and again by not keeping the terrorists behind bars. All of which meant the system couldn't be trusted this time, either.

That was why Gray had taken his day off to hike up the ridgeline, and it was why, even though he knew he should focus on returning Mawadi and the others to prison, in reality he wanted a far more permanent solution, and eye for an eye, a tooth for a tooth. Justice.

An image flashed in his head, a baby in a PICU incubator, her tiny hands clinging to her breathing tube just as tenaciously as she'd clung to life for twenty-two endless hours.

Keeping her memory in the forefront of his mind, Gray unclipped his holster and withdrew the 9 mm he'd carried on this little "hunting" trip, and started working his way through the trees, skirting the electric fence and the range of the motion detectors, heading for the back of the cabin.

The last of the surveillance reports, filed a few months earlier, had noted a rear exit, one that looked new, as though Mariah had put it in after she'd bought the cabin. Sure enough, there was a door at one end of the back of the building, with two windows beside it, blinds drawn to the sills. The rear exit was definitely a point in his favor, Gray decided. Mawadi and the others would have to power down the motion sensors when

their company arrived. In that small window of opportunity, Gray planned to slip in through the back.

If he could take Lee and his ex-wife alive, he would.
If not, dead was fine. He'd take his revenge however he
could get it.

MARIAH FOUGHT HER WAY through fuzzy, drugged layers
of consciousness and awoke to heart-pounding panic.
Twisting wildly against her bonds, she looked around
and found herself where she'd been the last time she'd
awakened: tied to her own bed in her otherwise
stripped-down bedroom. The nightstand and bureau
were gone, as were all her books and personal things.
That wasn't the worst of it, though. The worst was
knowing that although she'd woken up this time, it
didn't guarantee that she'd wake up the next.

Whenever she'd regained blurry consciousness over
the past few days, she'd seen Lee's face crowding close.
And she'd seen the murder in his eyes.

When the time came for her to die, she knew, he
would kill her himself, and he'd relish the process. He'd
delight in punishing her for having testified against
him, for helping break his alibi and for divorcing him
while he'd sat in jail. No doubt he would've already
killed her by now if it'd been up to him. It apparently
wasn't up to him, though. A second man had stood
behind him each time she'd awakened, his figure blurry
with distance and the drugs they had pumped into her
to keep her sedated for hours, maybe days.

Broad-shouldered and muscular, the second man
had dark, vaguely reptilian eyes. Lee had called him

Brisbane, though she didn't know if that was a first or last name, didn't think it mattered. The big man had arrived sometime between when Lee had drugged her unconscious and when she'd awakened the first time, lying on the floor in a pool of her own filth, still wearing the heavy layers and parka she'd had on when Lee attacked her. She must've made some noise when she'd regained consciousness, because she'd heard voices soon after, and Brisbane had come into the room.

At first she'd been terrified of the dark-eyed stranger with the faint accent, sure he was there to kill her. Instead, he'd been the one to keep Lee away from her— mostly, anyway—and he'd been the one who, when she'd begged, had untied her and let her shower and change her clothes. He'd watched her, cradling her shotgun in clear threat, but she'd forced herself through the process, shaking and crying, and weak with the drugs as she'd gulped shower water in a painful effort to slake her thirst.

She'd been almost grateful to collapse back onto her bed, have him retie her hands and feet, and let herself sink back into oblivion. She'd surfaced a few times after that; each time one of the men had untied her and let her use the bathroom, and once or twice she'd been given some sort of liquid protein shake that had made her gag as she'd forced it down. She'd been vaguely aware of questions and threats, aware of refusing to answer.

The last time, Lee had stayed behind after Brisbane left the room. She'd been seriously out of it, but had been aware enough to see the hatred in her ex-husband's eyes when he'd leaned over her. He'd wrapped one big, hurtful hand around her neck, squeezing lightly at first, then harder and harder, all the while staring down at her with those beautiful clear blue eyes of his, which made him look like a good guy, when he was anything but.

"I'll kill you for betraying me," he said, his voice as calm as if he'd been discussing the weather. "And for making me look bad. You should've answered questions when you had the chance. Now he's coming to *make* you talk." His eyes had slid to the door, and the quiet woods beyond. "As soon as we get what he needs from you, you're dead."

She hadn't needed to ask who *he* was; she'd known instinctively that it was al-Jihad. The terrorist leader was the one who'd given Lee a sense of purpose, though she hadn't known it at the time of their marriage. Al-Jihad was the one who'd told Lee to ingratiate himself into her life and use her father to gain inside information. Al-Jihad was also the one who'd told her husband to make sure she died in the bombings. And apparently he needed something more from her now. But what?

In a way, it didn't matter, because as Lee had leaned over her in her cabin bedroom, she'd seen her own murder in his eyes. One way or the other, she was dead.

She'd thought he was going to kill her right then, just choke the life out of her. He hadn't, though, and now she'd awakened yet again, bound to the wall, lying on her stripped-bare mattress. She thought it had been four, maybe five days since they'd imprisoned her. Five days that they'd kept her alive, feeding and watching over her because al-Jihad himself wanted something from her. She couldn't conceive of what it might be, though, couldn't remember the questions the men had asked her.

The cops and the Feds had taken everything that had belonged to Lee during their marriage, and she'd been glad to see it go. She'd given the rest of their things to charity, keeping only the few items she'd brought with her into the marriage, all keepsakes from her childhood. Nothing of any real value, and certainly nothing that would interest someone like al-Jihad. What could the terrorists possibly want?

The more her thoughts churned, the more Mariah's head cleared and the room sharpened around her. Her arms and legs tingled and nausea pounded low in her gut, but the rest of her felt nearly normal, suggesting that she was coming out of her drug-induced daze. Which was good news. But it was also bad news. Lee was too smart to let her regain consciousness unless he'd meant to, and she couldn't imagine that Brisbane was any less shrewd. So they'd intentionally let the drugs wear off, which suggested things were about the change. Was al-Jihad on his way up the mountain to question her personally? The idea was beyond terrifying. Al-Jihad was said to be an expert interrogator.

Nausea surged through Mariah, along with a rising buzz of adrenaline and the certainty that unless she got away now, she wouldn't be waking up ever again.

Stirring, she tried twisting on the bed. Her head spun, but her arms and legs moved when and where she told them to before hitting the ends of her bonds. Her ankles were crossed and tied with nylon rope, her hands bound behind her. A loop of rope ran from her feet to her wrists, and was threaded through an eyebolt screwed into one of the heavily varnished logs that made up the cabin wall.

She'd been lying in the same position for so long that her shoulders and hips had all but stopped aching, and had gone numb instead. As she moved, though, the tingling numbness started to recede, and pins and needles took over, making her hiss in pain. She gritted her teeth and kept going, pulling against her bonds, searching for some hint of give. The eyebolt and beam were solid, the bonds on her ankles tight enough to cut her skin. But after a few moments, she thought she felt the ropes on her wrists yield a little.

Excitement propelled her to work harder, and she yanked at the ropes, starting to breathe faster with the exertion. Blood moved through her veins with increasing force, and hope built alongside the panic that came at the thought that she was so close, but still might not get free in time.

"Come on, come on!" she muttered under her breath, working the ropes while straining to hear through the closed bedroom door. Was that a voice? A conversation? Or just the radio the men had been playing each time she'd awakened? Was that a footstep? Were they coming for her? Was it already too late?

The doorknob rattled and turned.

Mariah froze, holding her breath. The door opened a crack.

"Not yet," Brisbane said sharply from the other room. "They won't be here for another hour or so."

Lee's voice spoke from the doorway. "But I was just going to—"

"I know what you were going to do, and you're not doing it. You had your chance to question her, and it didn't work. Leave her be. We need her for another few hours. After al-Jihad's done with her, you can do whatever you want."

Mariah barely heard Lee's soft curse over the hammering of the pulse in her ears. But the door shut once again, and the footsteps moved away. She was saved—for the moment, anyway.

But time was running out.

Hurrying, nearly sobbing with terror, she fought against her bonds, yanking at the loosening ropes around her wrists and twisting against the tie connecting her hands and feet together. Slowly, ever so slowly, she worked her hands free from underneath the first layer of rope, then the second. The nylon strands cut into her skin and blood slicked her wrists, but she kept going, kept fighting, refusing to give up.

She'd given up before, accepting her marriage for what it was. Maybe she hadn't completely given up, but she'd certainly given in for too long, letting herself be blinded to the truth about her husband.

*Not again,* she vowed inwardly. *Not this time.*

On that thought, she gave a sharp jerk. Her left hand came free with a slash of pain as the nylon fibers tore into her skin. But she didn't care about the injury. She was free!

Working faster now, sobbing with fear, relief and excitement, she undid her other hand, then her feet. Rolling off the bed, she stood, barefoot and wobbly, wearing only the fleece sweatshirt and yoga pants Brisbane had tossed at her after her last shower. Within seconds, the crisp air inside the cabin cut through the single layer of material and chilled her skin, waking her further.

Trying not to think of how much colder it was going to be outside in the cool Colorado springtime, especially come nightfall, she headed for the door, keeping herself from passing out through sheer force of will. Two years ago she'd been too weak to deal with the downward spiral of her life. Now, hardened by time and Lee's betrayal, she was stronger. But was she strong enough?

"You're going to have to be," she whispered, saying the words aloud because the volume gave her growing resolution form and substance.

Brave words weren't going to get her out of the cabin, though. Not with the bedroom window nailed shut and two armed men in the front room, not to mention the motion detectors she'd so carefully wired in the woods around her home. They'd been meant to keep her safe. Now they would warn Lee and Brisbane if she managed to sneak out the back door. She didn't have her shotgun, didn't have the remote control to the security system, didn't have anything going for her except the knowledge that the men wanted her alive for another hour or two. They needed some sort of information from her, something important enough that they'd kept her alive and untouched for however many days it had been.

They might shoot at her, but they'd be aiming to wound, not kill. And everything she'd learned about firearms since this whole mess began suggested that it was very difficult to purposefully wound a fleeing target. During the trial it had come out that Lee had serious skill in bombmaking, but he'd claimed not to have any experience with guns. If she were lucky, Brisbane wouldn't be a sharpshooter, either. Even if he were, what was the difference, really?

Better to die trying to escape than let the terrorists use her to kill more innocents.

Mariah paused just shy of the doorway, feeling very small and alone. Raised by parents who'd met as rock band roadies and liked to keep moving, she'd lived in ten different places before her tenth birthday. Even after her parents had finally settled down in Bear Claw and her father had gone into engineering, landing a good job at the American Mall Group, Mariah had remained a private person, a loner who had to make a real effort when it came to meeting people. Her few forays into couplehood—including her disaster of a marriage—had only proved that she was the sort of person who was better off alone. Problem was, she wasn't always strong enough, smart enough, or just plain *enough* to do the things that needed to be done.

*You have no choice,* she told herself, clamping her lips together and fighting to be as silent as possible as she reached for the doorknob. Putting her ear to the panel, she listened intently but heard nothing, not even the radio. Did that mean both men were outside, maybe preparing for the arrival of the others? Or were they somewhere inside the cabin, just being quiet?

She didn't know, but she wasn't going to figure it out by listening at the door, either.

Blowing out a shallow, frightened breath, she eased the panel open and paused, tense and listening. Still no sound. She slipped through, unsteady on her numb legs, her heart beating so loud in her ears she was sure Lee and Brisbane would hear it all the way out front and come running.

But there was no shout of discovery as she slipped around the corner to the other back room, where she'd installed a rear door several months earlier. The room had served as her office; now it was overstuffed with the furniture Lee and Brisbane had pulled out of her bedroom, along with her usual office clutter. She glanced at her bureau, but it was facing the wall, which meant there was no way she could pull out clothes or shoes with any sort of stealth.

Crossing the room, barely breathing, she unlatched the dead bolt, wincing when the loud click cut through the silence. Then she opened the door and paused on the threshold, stalled by the sight of the fifty feet of raw-edged stumps between her and the relative safety of the forest.

Her heart thumped in her ears. She couldn't stay in the cabin. But crossing the clear-cut zone would trigger the alarms.

*They don't want me dead,* she reminded herself, although that was little solace as she drew a deep breath, plucked up her thin courage and plunged through the door.

She hit the ground running. Splinters and woodchips

from the clear-cutting bit into her feet, but she kept going. Seconds later, the alarms went off, emitting a mechanized buzz that sliced through the air and straight through to her soul.

She wanted to scream but held the sound in, hoping to delay discovery as long as possible. Maybe they weren't even home. Maybe they'd gone to meet—

"She's out. Get her!" Lee's shout warned that she wasn't that lucky.

Moments later, a shotgun blasted behind her, and a full pellet load blew out the top of a nearby stump as she ran past it. The next shot hit the ground behind her, stinging the backs of her calves with dirt spray.

The pain worried Mariah that she'd miscalculated, badly. Apparently, they'd rather have her dead than free.

She screamed once in fear, but then clamped her lips on further cries. She wouldn't give up! Sobbing, she flung herself the rest of the way across the clear-cut zone and hurdled the low electric line with ill grace.

She landed hard, stumbled and went to her knees, her legs burning with injury and exertion. As she fell, the shotgun roared, and tree bark exploded right where her head had just been.

Blubbering, she rolled and scrambled back up, then ran for her life as Lee and Brisbane bolted across the clearing and plunged into the forest after her. The alarms cut out abruptly. She heard the men's curses and their heavy, crashing footsteps. They were close. Too close!

She didn't dare loop around to the vehicles at the

front of the cabin; she couldn't trust that the keys would be in plain sight or that her captors hadn't created some sort of roadblock farther down the lane. So she ran the other way, deeper into the forest, limping on her badly abraded feet, but unable to slow down for her injuries. Her breath sobbed in her lungs, burning with each inhalation, and wetness streamed down her face, a mix of tears, sweat and panic.

"There!" Brisbane shouted from her right. "Over there! For crap's sake, get her!"

Brush crashed, the noises closer now and gaining on her. Mariah kept going, but her body was weak; her legs had gone to jelly and her feet and calves screamed in pain. She stumbled, dragged herself up and stumbled again. This time she went down and hit the ground hard. For a second, she lay there, stunned.

Before she could recover, rough hands grabbed her.

Panic assailed her and she started to struggle, inhaled to scream, but someone clapped a hand across her mouth and hissed, "Quiet!"

Then the world lurched and he was dragging her, lifting her and wrestling her into what looked like a solid wall of thorny brush from a distance, but up close proved to be scrub covering a deep depression, where a tree had fallen and the root ball had popped up, forming an earthen cave of sorts.

Excitement speared through Mariah alongside confusion. She looked back and got an impression of a square-jawed soldier wearing a thick woolen cap, heavy, insulated camouflage clothing and no insignia. He wasn't Lee or Brisbane. He was…rescuing her?

He shoved her into the hiding spot and crowded in behind her.

"Down," he whispered tersely, pressing her into the cold, moist earth and following her, rolling partway on top of her so she was beneath him and they were pressed back-to-front, with his heavy weight all but squeezing the breath from her lungs.

The fallen tree had rotted over time, providing nourishment for the profusion of vines and scrub plants that had sprung from it, forming an almost impenetrable thicket. But would it be enough to conceal them fully?

Her rescuer's arms tightened around her, and he breathed in her ear, "Be very still. They'll see us if you move."

Coming from nearby, she heard the sound of footsteps in the undergrowth, and a man's muttered curse. Freezing, Mariah pressed herself flat beneath the soldier, and held her breath, praying they wouldn't be discovered.

The noises stopped ten, maybe fifteen feet away. After a moment, Lee's voice called, "Are you sure you saw her? There's nothing here."

"She was there a second ago. Keep looking." Brisbane's answer came from the other side of the woods, back toward the cabin. After a moment, Lee moved off.

Mariah counted her heartbeats, trying to stay calm as she exhaled slowly, then risked inhaling a breath. Another. The sounds of the search diminished slightly, suggesting that the men had moved to the other side of the cabin.

Hoping that Lee and Brisbane were walking into

one hell of an ambush, she rolled her eyes back, trying to get a look at her rescuer as she mouthed, "Where are the others hiding?"

He must be part of a coordinated attack, right? Somehow, someone had learned that she was in trouble and had sent help.

Most likely, the FBI agents—particularly the cold, gray-eyed bastard who'd kept questioning her father even after he'd started complaining of chest pains—had been keeping watch on the cabin. They'd probably identified Lee days ago and were just now moving in, knowing al-Jihad was on his way. The thought that they'd known she was in there and hadn't bothered to mount a rescue beforehand brought a kick of resentment, but it was no more than she'd come to expect from the Feds. They carried out their own plans on their own timetable, and to hell with the people they hurt in the process.

But the soldier shook his head slightly. "I'm alone," he breathed in her ear. "Quiet now. They're coming back."

*What?* Mariah's thoughts churned. It didn't make any sense that he'd be up on the ridgeline alone, but she couldn't deny the physical reality of him, either. She would've demanded an explanation, but just then, Brisbane and Lee returned, stopping very close to the thick copse where Mariah and the soldier were hidden. The two men conferred in low voices.

Breathing shallowly through her mouth, Mariah flattened herself against the moist, partially rotted leaves and twigs beneath her. She was acutely aware of the man pressed against her. The solid weight of him was more reassuring than it probably should have been, and she fought the urge to huddle her chilled body into his heavy warmth as her mind continued to race.

What sort of soldier worked alone?

"I'll call down and have the boss bring up more men," Lee said. "We'll fan out, search every rock and tree until we find her. The bitch has to be hiding somewhere nearby—there's no way she got away that fast with no shoes."

"I told you to keep her drugged," Brisbane spat, disgusted. "Told you she was smarter than you gave her credit for."

Lee's voice edged toward a whine. "I thought al-Jihad would prefer her awake."

"Awake doesn't do us any good if she's gone. This was your idea. At this point, you'd better hope to hell she doesn't make it down the ridge, or your ass is toast."

"Al-Jihad wouldn't do anything to me. He needs me."

"Al-Jihad doesn't need anybody," Brisbane countered. "Come on, let's keep looking. I'll start over here while you call down and tell the others we need a full-fledged search party. Have them bring up infrared, night vision, the whole works. They'll want to watch the roads, too. The bitch is bound to turn up somewhere."

Despite the warm weight of the man pressed against her, Mariah began to shiver, fear and confusion warring within her. What did they want from her? Whatever they wanted, the men were right about one thing: in the absence of help, it seemed highly unlikely that she'd make it to safety—the nights were too cold, the trails difficult to manage without proper climbing equipment, never mind without shoes of any kind. If she had help, though, she might very well make it off the ridge and into the city safely.

Question was, did the man who held her count as help?

As Lee and Brisbane moved off in opposite directions, the sounds of their steps fading to forest silence, she stirred beneath the stranger, twisting around to get a good look at him. "Who are—" She bit off the question with a quiet hiss when she recognized the cool gray eyes beneath the woolen cap, recognized the suit-clad monster in the man she'd thought was a soldier. *"Grayson!"* She spat the word out like a curse.

It was Special Agent Michael Grayson, the FBI agent who'd made her life a living hell and nearly killed her father in his efforts to get at a truth that had existed only in his mind.

And now she was at his mercy.

## Chapter Three

"I prefer to be called Gray. Not that it matters much to you, I'm guessing," he said, seeing displeasure flood her face, no doubt due to the way he'd treated her and her family during the investigation. Which was too bad, because as far as he was concerned he'd done what needed to be done.

Besides, it wasn't as if he was thrilled to see her, either. He hadn't been about to let Mawadi grab her and drag her back inside, but rescuing her had complicated the hell out of the situation. He'd planned to wait for the five o'clock meet and move in then, when the motion detectors were down, but now there were going to be more men, and they would be searching the damn forest, which shot that plan to shreds.

No, the best thing for him to do now would be to get the woman down to the city and hand her over to Johnson and his crew. The SAC would be furious that Gray had disobeyed orders, but he'd be forced to send a team up to the cabin. Gray knew damn well that by the time they got up to the ridgeline, Mawadi and the others would be long gone. But, unfortunately, as tough as Gray might be, he was just was one man with a 9 mm, and that was no match for a terrorist cell on high alert.

Muttering a curse, he rolled off the woman, banishing the sensory memory of how she'd felt beneath him—all soft, curvy and female. He so wasn't going there.

Once this was all over and al-Jihad and the others had been brought to justice, he'd allow himself to live again. But at the moment he had no intention of letting himself be distracted by a woman. Besides, even if he had the inclination, there was no way in hell he'd be going for this woman. There was a physical connection, yes—it had been there from the first moment he saw her. But she was a witness at best, a conspirator at worst, and she'd been married to one of the bombers.

She was a means to an end, nothing more. The fact that her glare suggested that she hated his guts made it that much easier to ignore the fine buzz of tension running through his body as they faced each other in their small hiding space.

Her eyes were dark and bruised in her pale face, her full lips trembling, though whether from fear or cold or a combination of the two, he didn't know. It didn't much matter, either, because he needed to focus on getting them the hell away from the cabin and down to cell phone range ASAP.

Shucking out of his camo jacket, he shoved it at the woman. "There are mittens in the pocket. Put them on your feet and follow me. And for crap's sake, don't make any noise."

She started to snap in response, but shut her mouth when he pulled his gun from where he'd tucked it at the small of his back, and racked the action to the ready position, just in case.

He waited for a second, watching to see what she was going to do. When she pulled on the jacket without comment, then felt in the pocket and covered her bloody feet as best she could with the mittens, he nodded grimly. "Good call."

Then he turned his back on her and led the way out of the small copse, moving as silently as he could, but traveling fast because the light was fading. Already, the sky had gone gray-blue, and the world around them had turned colorless with the approaching spring dusk. So he jog-trotted downhill, hoping to hell they'd get lucky and make it down the ridgeline undetected.

The first half mile was tough going through a hilly section of deadfall-choked forest, made more difficult by the fading light. At first Mariah moved quietly, but as they kept going, Gray heard her breathing start to labor, heard her miss her footing more and more often.

He turned back, ready to snap at her to be quiet if she wanted to live. But one look at her waxy, pale face, which had gone nearly white in the fading light, had him biting back the oath and cursing himself instead.

He crossed the small gap between them and caught her as she crumpled, sweeping her up against his chest.

She was feather-light in his arms, though his memory said she'd been solid, bordering on sturdy before. The change nagged at him, making him wonder exactly how long she'd been bound in that cabin, and what Mawadi and the other man had done to her.

Guilt pinched, but Gray quickly shoved it aside, into the mental refuse bin where he consigned his other useless emotions, few and far between though they might be.

After only a few seconds of unconsciousness, she roused against him, pushing feebly at his chest. Her eyes fluttered open. The dusk robbed them of their color, but he knew they were amber, just as he knew he couldn't trust the stealthy twist of heat that curled through his midsection when their gazes locked. She moistened her lips and swallowed, and he was far too aware of those simple actions, just as he was far too susceptible to the tremor in her voice when she whispered, "Put me down. I can walk."

"Don't be stupid," he said, the words coming out more roughly than he'd intended. He yanked his gaze from hers and pressed her closer, not in comfort, but so he wouldn't be looking at her face, wouldn't be thinking of how her body felt against his, flaring unwanted heat at the points of contact.

Gritting his teeth, he shifted his grip so he could shove the 9 mm back in the small of his spine, then took hold of her once again and headed downhill, moving as fast as he could while still keeping quiet. His four-by-four was maybe another mile farther down, and as he hiked, he forced himself to focus on the case, not the woman. The case was important. The woman wasn't.

By now, Mawadi and the second man would have gotten in touch with the other members of their cell. If Gray could talk SAC Johnson into sending choppers and search teams up to the cabin, they might get lucky. They wouldn't get al-Jihad, of course; he was too smart to come up the mountain now. But they might get Mawadi, might get some idea of why the terrorists had returned to the area.

As Gray put one boot in front of the other and his back and arms began to ache, though, it wasn't the terrorists, his boss or even revenge that occupied his mind—it was the woman in his arms. And that could become a problem if he let it.

MARIAH WOULD HAVE held herself away from Gray, but she lacked the strength to do anything but cling, with one arm looped over his neck and her face pressed into the warm hollow at his throat. She despised surrendering control to him, hated that her safety was in the hands of the FBI special agent who had been a large part of making her life a living hell more than two years earlier, and whose relentless questions had put her father in the hospital, nearly in his grave.

But at the same time, the man who held her easily, walking with long, powerful strides, was so unlike the picture in her mind, it was causing her brain to jam. This man was warm to the touch rather than cold, and when their eyes had met, his had blazed with an emotion that she couldn't define, but had been far from the detached, sardonic chill he'd projected during the investigation.

His warmth and steady masculine scent surrounded her now, coming from the jacket he'd given her and from the solid wall of his body against hers. She'd hated the man who had interrogated her, hated what he stood for and how he treated people. But she didn't know how to feel about the man he'd turned out to be—the soldier who'd come up to her cabin alone and had been there when she'd needed him in a way that nobody else had for a long, long time.

Confused, weak with drugs and exhaustion, she was unable to do anything but give in to circumstances beyond her immediate control. Closing her eyes, she leaned into her rescuer, anchoring herself to his warmth and strength.

She must've dozed—or maybe passed out—after that. She was vaguely aware of Gray loading her into a large vehicle and strapping her in tightly. Through the fuzzed-out fog her brain had become, she knew that he was white-knuckle tense as he pulled the vehicle out of its hiding spot and headed it down the road. It was full dark; he wore a pair of night-vision goggles he'd retrieved from the glove compartment and drove with the truck's headlights off, muttering a string of curses under his breath as he kept the gas pedal down and steered the vehicle along the fire-access road leading down from her cabin. Then they flew through the gate, which hung open, and turned onto the paved road headed toward Bear Claw.

He decelerated, shucked off the goggles and flipped on the headlights before glancing over at her. "We got lucky. No sign of your husband's reinforcements."

"Ex-husband," she corrected him, the faint echoes of warmth and gratitude dispelled by irritation because he'd made the same mistake a handful of times during the initial investigation into the prison break. It annoyed her that he kept insisting on the undoubtedly deliberate gaffe, and that she couldn't stop herself from correcting him each time.

He nodded, his eyes not quite the cold steel of Special Agent Grayson, not quite the fiery resolve of the soldier he'd been up on the ridgeline. When his gaze met hers, she felt a click of unwanted connection and a shimmer of fear. *What next?* she wanted to ask him, but didn't, because she wasn't sure she wanted to know what his answer would be.

So, instead, she turned away from him, settling into her seat as the truck accelerated, heading for the city. While he drove, he made a call on his cell, tersely reporting the situation, and what he'd seen and done. Mariah didn't add anything to the conversation. There was nothing she could do to change her situation; she was too weak, too confused. And, bottom line: whether it was logical or not, she was heart-sore.

Being around Lee again hadn't only been terrifying, it had also brought to the surface of her mind things that she'd thought she'd managed to bury years ago. Seeing him had reminded her of the good times—or at least the times she'd thought were good ones, when Lee had courted her. He'd brought her flowers and silly gifts; he'd made her feel as though she were the center of his universe, that she was special. And when he'd proposed, dropping to one knee and promising that they would be together forever, she'd believed him.

But those memories were overlaid now with the pain of remembering the months after their marriage, when he'd gradually changed, growing cold and distant. After a while, his petty cruelties and outright manipulations had made her grateful for the nights he didn't come home, and had made her start to think she was losing her mind. It was only later that she realized that he'd purposely broken her down, little by little, undermining the defenses she'd built up over a lifetime of being an outsider. Then, once he'd made her completely vulnerable by promising her forever, he'd started beating her down further, stripping her of her worth until she'd been nothing but his wife, his plaything. Simply because he could, because it amused him.

She knew the authorities thought of Lee as a follower, a patsy. She knew different; he might follow al-Jihad's orders, but when it had come to their marriage, he'd been the one in control.

Despite the months of subtle torment, though, she'd retained a tiny core of strength. It had been too little, too late back then. Would it be enough to see her through whatever came next?

The bang of a car door startled her, jolting her awake, though she hadn't realized that she'd been dozing.

She squinted against the sudden glare of lights. When she finally focused on the scene, she recognized the walled-in parking lot of the main police station in Bear Claw City. A tingle of unease and ill will shimmered through her at the memories of being interrogated in the station, then rushing her father to the nearby hospital, where he'd nearly died, not just because of Gray's heavy-handed questioning, but because of the decisions Mariah herself had made, the horror she'd brought into her parents' lives.

That was her shame. One of many.

There was a crowd gathering outside the truck; it seemed to be made up of equal parts cops and suited-up Feds, with the latter group gathering around Gray as he climbed from the vehicle. In his flannel shirt and camouflage pants, with his short brown hair bristled on end and his face and clothing streaked with dirt and sweat, mute testimony of their harrowing escape, he should've looked at a disadvantage compared to the other agents, neat and clean in their dark suits. To Mariah's eye, though, he looked like a man of action, one who could break the others in half, and might do just that, given the provocation.

She saw him visibly brace himself as he squared off opposite a salt-and-pepper-haired agent who wore an air of command and a deep scowl. It took Mariah a moment to place the other man, but when she did, nerves bunched in her midsection.

SAC Johnson, the FBI special agent in charge of the federal arm of the jailbreak investigation, had struck her as a pompous ass far more concerned with his own on-camera image than the actual investigation. There was no way she wanted him calling the shots when it came to her cabin…and potentially her life. Because that was one of the things that seemed painfully clear: she didn't need to protect herself simply from Lee's personal revenge. The terrorists apparently wanted something from her, which meant she was going to need help staying safe, whether she liked it or not.

Not liking it one bit, she pushed open the truck door, unclipped her seat belt and dropped down from the vehicle, hissing in pain when she landed on her injured feet.

A young, uniformed Bear Claw City cop appeared at her side almost instantly, and took her arm. "This way, ma'am. Agent Grayson said you're wounded. We have an EMT-trained officer who'll take a look at you while we wait for the paramedics."

"Not yet." She pulled away, focused on the group of FBI special agents, where Gray and SAC Johnson were arguing in low voices, their faces set in stone.

She took a couple of hobbling steps toward the knot of suits, pulling Gray's camouflage jacket more tightly around her shoulders. As she came closer, she heard Johnson snarl, "Were my orders somehow unclear?"

"No, sir." Gray's square jaw was locked, his eyes cool. But underneath that coolness, Mariah thought she sensed an undercurrent of hot anger. For the first time, she started to wonder whether the chill of his demeanor was designed to hide something entirely different, something more in line with the soldier he'd been up on the ridgeline.

*And you so shouldn't be thinking about that right now,* Mariah told herself as she moved to join the men.

Johnson glared at his subordinate. "So my orders were clear, yet you deliberately disobeyed them by performing reconnaissance near Ms. Shore's cabin."

Gray nodded. "Yes, sir."

Which explained why he'd been alone. It also reinforced her initial impression that Johnson was more focused on protocol than results, whereas Gray was… well, she didn't know what he was, but he wasn't anything like his boss.

"If Agent Grayson hadn't been up at the cabin, acting on orders or not, I'd probably be dead by now," Mariah said, coming up beside Gray. "And you wouldn't have a clue that Lee and the others are back in the area, would you?" When the older man's attention locked on her and his scowl deepened, Mariah lifted her chin and met his glare.

Johnson must've seen something in her eyes, because he brought his attitude down a notch, nodding and holding out a hand. "You may not remember me, Ms. Shore. I'm Special Agent in Charge Johnson."

"I remember." She shook because there was no reason not to, then said, "Please tell me that you have men on their way to my cabin."

"They're already on scene. The cabin shows signs of having been abandoned in a hurry."

Gray bit off a curse. "You searched the woods?"

"Of course. Mawadi and the others are gone."

"What about—" Gray began.

"The investigation is proceeding appropriately," Johnson interrupted with a sharp look in Gray's direction. "That's all Ms. Shore needs to know." He returned his attention to Mariah. "Obviously, we'll need to ask you some questions."

Mariah nodded. "Of course."

She hoped none of them could tell how much she dreaded the next few hours, how much she wished she could rewind time by a week, to when she'd been at home in her cabin, safe in her delusion that Lee couldn't get at her there. But she wasn't back in her cabin. She was smack in the middle of the city, in enemy territory.

She'd dealt with the FBI's idea of "some questions" twice before. The first time, she'd been weak and soft, and they'd bullied her and her parents until they'd nearly broken. The second time, just after the jailbreak, she'd been in shock, dazed and disconnected, and her flat affect had put her under suspicion, making them think she was hiding something, maybe even that she'd been in contact with Lee. In the aftermath of that second round of questioning, she'd vowed never to make those mistakes again, never to be the victim again.

Lee might have captured and victimized her, but she wasn't his victim, wasn't anyone's victim. If the agents wanted something from her, they could damn well give something back this time.

So she met Johnson's eyes and said, "I'll tell you everything I know, but I have conditions."

Beside her, Gray muttered a bitter oath, but she couldn't take her eyes off his boss, couldn't correct what she suspected was a deep misapprehension. There would be time for that later. Maybe.

There was no humor to the wry twist of Johnson's lips. "Of course you do." He paused, waving over two uniformed officers.

Mariah stiffened when they flanked her and urged her away from the agents, away from Gray. "Wait!" she cried, unconsciously reaching for him.

Gray drew away, and when he looked down at her, his eyes had gone even colder than before. He said, "They're taking you inside where it's safer, and where they can clean up your injuries, find you some shoes and socks, and something else to wear. They'll get you some food, something to drink. I'd advise you to take them up on the offer. I have a feeling it's going to be a long night for all of us."

Even wearing camouflage, he'd gone back to being the no-nonsense agent she remembered, and she hated the change. But in a way it was a good thing, because it forced her to step away from him, made her remember that they weren't friends, that there was no real connection between them. He might have gotten her off the ridgeline, but that didn't make him her white knight.

She nodded and took a big step back. "Thanks for the rescue," she said, which didn't even begin to encompass what she was feeling just then.

His eyes went hooded. "Sorry I didn't get there a couple of days earlier." He turned away before she could process the flicker of emotion she thought she'd seen in his eyes, the one that suggested she wasn't alone in feeling a spark of attraction where none should exist.

Part of her wanted to ask him to stay with her, but what sense did that make? He might have rescued her, and he might have disobeyed orders in the process, but that didn't mean he was on her side. Far from it, in fact. Because how could she forget what he'd done to her father? Gray had hammered at him with the same questions over and over again, implying that her father had known about Lee's plan, that she and her whole family had knowingly helped the terrorists. Which was so wrong it should've sounded preposterous, only it hadn't, coming from him. And as the first hour had turned to three, he hadn't eased up, hadn't given up, even when her father's color had started to fade. Eventually, he'd let them go, but not without a stern warning to stay available, that there would be more questions to come.

By nightfall, her father had been in the cardiac ICU. By the next day, he'd been undergoing bypass surgery. All because of a not-so-civil servant on a mission to uncover an imaginary conspiracy. In the same vein, Gray had been up on the ridgeline, not to rescue her, but because he'd been suspicious of her. Again.

She couldn't trust him, couldn't lean on him. And she'd do well to remember that.

Chest aching with a hollow sense of disappointment she knew she shouldn't feel, Mariah turned to Johnson. "As I said, I'll cooperate, but I've got conditions."

"We'll see." He gestured to the men flanking her. "Take her inside, let her clean up and call counsel. I'll be there in fifteen."

The uniformed cops escorted her to a small, spare room where a pair of paramedics waited for her, equipment at the ready. One was a pretty, light-haired woman with kind eyes; the other an older, heavyset man who looked like he'd rather be napping.

Mariah held up both hands. "It's not all that bad, really. Just some cuts on my feet, and a pellet-burn on my calves." And a hell of a headache, and some serious room spins, thanks to the residue of whatever Lee and Brisbane had been pumping into her system. When she listed it like that, she started to feel worse by the second.

The light-haired woman shook her head apologetically. "We'll treat your injuries, for sure. But first the

CSIs want to collect your clothes and photograph you. We'll need a blood sample, too."

Two and a half years earlier, Mariah would have— and had—done whatever the cops had asked. Older and wiser now out of necessity, she said, "Then I'm going to want to call my lawyer first."

She was done being a pushover.

OVER THE NEXT EIGHTEEN hours, Gray fought to get himself put back on the case and lost, fought to keep his active-duty status and lost that battle, too. Johnson was furious that he'd disobeyed orders. More importantly, the SAC was embarrassed that Gray's breach of protocol had yielded a badly needed break in the case. As far as Johnson was concerned, the new intel didn't cancel out Gray's insubordination, not after he'd been specifically warned to stay away from Mariah.

Those conversations took place in snatches, amid the information storm that followed the new developments. The response team reported back with little new information from the cabin, and the infrared helicopter sweeps failed to turn up anything but wildlife and a few hardy preseason campers up on the ridgeline. There was no sign of Lee Mawadi or the other man, whom Mariah hadn't yet identified from among al-Jihad's known associates. More, although Mariah was convinced Lee had tried to question her, and had called al-Jihad for help when she'd proven resistant, she claimed to have no idea what they wanted from her.

It was possible that the forthcoming detailed forensic analysis of the cabin might yield some clue as to where the terrorists were going, where they'd come from or what they wanted with Mariah. However, it would be days at the earliest—more likely weeks—before the relevant clues were teased out from among the normal detritus of a lived-in home. The Bear Claw crime scene analysts were excellent, and had strong ties to the federal investigators, but they weren't miracle workers.

Meanwhile, the members of the prison break task force, who had scattered over the past months when the investigation had moved away from Bear Claw, were being reassembled. As before, the investigation would be headquartered partly at the FBI's Denver field office, partly at the Bear Claw City PD. However, Gray wouldn't be part of the task force at either location. Johnson had made it crystal clear that he didn't want to work with a renegade, couldn't afford to risk a court appeal if one of his agents used questionable methods during an investigation. The SAC had offered Gray a transfer or a desk to ride, but they both knew he wouldn't take either. The offer had been an empty formality, nothing more.

Which was why, at just past noon on the day after he'd rescued Mariah and broken the news that Lee Mawadi was back in town, Gray was in his Denver office, packing his personal effects. His service weapon and badge were on the desk, weighting down his letter of resignation.

He didn't feel grief at the decision, didn't feel relief. He felt hollow. Determined. He might be off the task force, but he wasn't off the case. Not by a long shot.

He piled his things haphazardly into a box, leaving

the official stuff behind and taking only the few items he cared about. The first was a bifold frame containing a picture of his parents and him at his academy gradua- tion a decade earlier on one side, opposite a more recent shot of his whole extended family, cousins and all, taken last Christmas. The latter photo brought a spear of the pain he suspected would always accompany thoughts of the holidays, but he hadn't let that keep him away from family doings. Christmas was important to his parents, and therefore it was important to him. He'd gone to the annual get-together and pretended to enjoy himself, and had ducked the inevitable questions about his love life, reminding himself that his family members meant no harm. Even though most of them were cops or married to cops, they didn't fully understand that he had things to take care of before he could move on.

Thinking of those things, he set the bifold frame in the box and picked up a smaller photo of a laughing man grinning up at the camera, his arms wrapped around a flushed-faced woman who held a small baby.

"Grayson," SAC Johnson's voice barked from the doorway, stanching the impending flood of memories and setting Gray's teeth on edge.

Gray didn't even look over at his soon-to-be-ex boss, just placed the photo in the cardboard box and gestured to the pile of papers on his desk. "The letter of resig- nation's right there. Go away."

"I want you to reconsider."

Of all the things Gray might've expected, that didn't even make the list. Frowning, he turned toward Johnson.

And saw Mariah standing behind him.

She looked very different than she had the day before. Her dark hair fell to her shoulders in soft waves, and she wore a green turtleneck sweater, jeans and boots that made her look like a model out of an upscale outdoorsy catalog, simultaneously sexy and practical.

Although he'd always before gravitated to fussy, feminine women, Gray felt something inside him go very still and hushed, the way it did just before he got the "go" signal on a major op, when his body was poised equally between fight and flight, his blood surging with adrenaline and survival instincts. This wasn't an op or a fight, he knew, but he had a feeling that if he let it, his association with Mariah could become just as messy. So it was up to him not to let it go there.

Straightening, he nodded to her. "Mariah."

"Gray," she acknowledged, her expression giving away nothing. She pushed past Johnson, then hesitated just inside the office doorway. "I need to talk to you." She threw a look over her shoulder and said pointedly, "Alone."

Johnson muttered something under his breath, but nodded. He shot Gray a warning look, one that said, "For crap's sake, don't screw this up," then retreated, shutting the door at Mariah's back.

A tense, anticipatory silence filled the small room until Gray broke it by grabbing the box top off his desk and fitting it into place, sealing in the memories. "I expect Johnson told you that I don't work here anymore."

"Yes. Right after I told him I'd let the FBI use me to set a trap for Lee, but only if you act as my bodyguard."

Gray had thought he was beyond surprise when it came to this case. Apparently, he was wrong. "Why me?"

"Because you don't play Johnson's game."

That got his attention. "What game would that be?"

She was still standing just inside the door, as though she might slip away at any moment. She didn't leave, though, didn't move a muscle. She just stood there, her eyes locked with his, as though she were trying to figure out how much to tell him, how much to trust him. After a short pause, she said, "The game where he does and says exactly the right thing, the defensible, by-the-book thing, even when it's the wrong choice under the circumstances. Let me guess…he wants to be governor some day."

"Actually, I'm pretty sure he's got his sights set on Congress." Gray was reluctantly impressed, though. Not too many people saw through the SAC's act, at least not until they'd known him for a while. Moving around the desk, he crossed the room to stand very near her, close enough that he could see the flutter of her pulse at her throat. "You want me guarding you because my boss doesn't like me. Any other reason? Not to pry, but I didn't get the impression you liked me very much, either, especially after what happened with your father two years ago."

"That wasn't your fault," she said, surprising him again. At his startled look, she glanced away. "I didn't get much sleep last night, for obvious reasons. It gave me an opportunity to think a few things through. One of the conclusions I came to was that the outcome would've been the same even if you'd been all sweetness and light in the interview. My father was furious with himself for not seeing Lee for what he was. He was in the process of being forcibly retired from his company because of his involvement in the bombings, and he was trying to deal with a boatload of guilt. The interrogation just brought all that to the forefront at once, and his heart couldn't take it."

Something in her voice suggested that wasn't the whole story, but Gray didn't call her on it. Instead, he cleared his throat and waited for her to focus on him. Then he said, "For what it's worth, I'm sorry about how it played out." He'd called the hospital to check on her father, but didn't think she needed to know that. In a way it'd probably be better if she saw him as the enemy, especially since he was getting the idea that they hadn't yet seen the last of each other. Still, he found himself asking, "How's he doing?"

That earned him a sharp look, but she must've seen that his question was sincere, because she answered civilly enough. "He had a second surgery a few months ago. I guess he's doing okay now."

"You guess?" When she didn't respond, he pressed, "Are you afraid that this is going to set his recovery back?" By *this,* he meant her imprisonment and the continued situation with Mawadi, and indicated as much by sketching a wave around his office, ending with his badge, which lay on his desk beside his resignation letter.

She shook her head. "My parents moved away last year, said they were done with Colorado." The way she said it made it sound like Colorado wasn't the only thing they'd turned their backs on.

"I'm sorry."

"Not your fault."

They fell silent, and in the quiet he became aware of how close he and Mariah were standing. He could feel her warmth reaching out to him, making him itch to be even closer still, to lift a hand to her face and touch her. To kiss her.

Before the mad impulse could supersede his better judgment, he said, "What, exactly, do you want from me?"

"Johnson is going to arrange to have me hospitalized, and let it leak that I was found on the ridgeline. I want you to be in charge of surveillance, and when Lee comes for me, I want you to take care of him."

"Take care of him?" The idea of killing Mawadi in cold blood didn't bother Gray nearly as much as it probably should have.

"Get him off the streets and out of my life," she said, which wasn't really a clarification. "And in the process, I want you to do your best to keep me alive." There was a new thread of steel in her voice when she said, "I know you'll do whatever it takes—rules or no rules. Since that's the way Lee thinks, it's the only way you're going to be able to take him down before he gets what he wants from me, and undoubtedly uses it to kill again. Your boss doesn't understand that, which is why I want you involved." She held out her hand. "What do you say?"

He looked at her for a long moment, seeing her outstretched hand and the delicate bones of her wrist, which he could break one-handed if he wanted to. But though her bone structure might be more delicate than he'd remembered—made especially prominent now by her days in captivity—the woman herself was far stronger than he'd thought. He saw it in her eyes and heard it in her voice.

The part of him that still spent the holidays with his family, knowing it mattered to them, said he should decline, that he should put Mariah into protective custody, stay on the job and do whatever he could—or rather whatever Johnson would let him do—to bring Lee Mawadi, al-Jihad and the others to justice through official means.

But the other part of him, the part that awakened from nightmares drenched in sweat, seized with killing rage and the need for revenge—that part had him reaching out and gripping her hand. As he shook on it, he felt a twinge of guilt and regret, a premonition that pretty Mariah Shore would be the one to suffer the most from her choices.

In the end, though, he knew that nothing else mattered but getting justice for the dead. He was a little surprised to find that she knew it, too.

"Okay," he said softly. "I'll do it."

# Chapter Four

Over the next two days, Mariah learned that it was far easier to say "Use me as bait" than it was to actually *be* the so-called bait.

Gray and the others had installed her in a square private hospital room that embodied the word *drab*. The furniture was cheap prefab; the upholstery, paint and uninspired wall art were all variations on the same theme of beige, mauve and mossy green. The single window overlooked the parking lot and was on a low floor, so she couldn't even see beyond the neighboring buildings to the mountains in the distance. Not that she'd even seen much of the parking lot, because Gray had ordered her to stay in bed, aside from necessary trips to the small bathroom located in a walled-off corner of the room. They had no way of knowing the sophistication level of al-Jihad's local network, so she had to play the part of an invalid.

Round-the-clock guards stood outside her door, but they were mostly for the show of protective custody, and were on orders to let their vigilance slip now and then for a bathroom break or conversation. Mariah's real security came from electronic surveillance that had been installed in secret by a team dressed to look like a maintenance crew. Thanks to them, she was constantly being monitored by both video and audio. Hello, Big Brother.

Five years earlier, when she'd moved to New York, full of hope and enthusiasm, bursting with plans to launch herself into the world of fashion photography while becoming part of the "in" crowd, she might've seen the hidden cameras and microphones as no big deal; she'd tried out for that reality show, hadn't she? But that period of her life had been a fluke, an aberration. She'd been trying to make herself into someone bright, glittering and interesting, someone very unlike the shy, uprooted loner she'd been throughout high school and college.

And for a time, she'd succeeded.

It had been during that time that she'd met Lee—or rather, he'd arranged to meet her. For the months he'd been courting her, she'd truly felt like the bright, glittering, interesting person she was trying to be. But she hadn't been bright and interesting, she'd been desperate for attention, and so gullible that she'd bought his act right down to the last "I love you." She'd thought it was her idea to move to Bear Claw in an effort to forge a better relationship with her parents, her idea for her father to help Lee get a job. In reality, she'd been played, and played badly.

She hadn't been glittery or interesting. Worse, she'd been stupid. In retrospect, it seemed ludicrous that she'd ever believed that a man like the one Lee had portrayed could have been interested in her, never mind being smitten, as he'd claimed to be. She simply wasn't the type to inspire strong emotions in other people. Not her parents, not men, not anyone.

Drifting in her hospital bed, dozing in that half-aware state between sleeping and waking, she thought of the hopes and dreams she'd brought into her marriage, and how Lee had extinguished them one by one.

As if summoned by the memories, she heard his voice in her mind, low and beguiling. *You're going to help us whether you like it or not,* he'd whispered against her cheek, his breath feathering the hair at her temple as she'd lain bound and helpless, slipping into drugged oblivion. *It's simple, really, all you have to do is tell me where—*

"Deep thoughts?" Gray's low, masculine voice said, breaking the reverie.

Mariah jolted alert, yanking her attention to the doorway of her drab hospital room even as she scrambled to hold on to the memory. Or had it even been a memory? She wasn't sure, didn't know if it would help even if it had been real. Confusion churned through her, and it didn't dissipate one iota at the sight of Gray standing there. If anything, her tension increased, not because she was afraid of him, or even because of the misplaced resentment she'd harbored against him for far too long.

No, this tension was purely a product of the situation and the man.

Deciding to keep the partially remembered whisper to herself for the moment, she shook her head and answered his question with a neutral, "Just resting."

His gray suit hung on him a little, disguising the broad shoulders, flat waist and strong legs she now knew were part of the package. He looked as though he'd lost weight since he'd bought the clothes, making her think that in the past he might have carried some softness that was no longer evident in his tough, honed frame. That same toughness edged the sharp planes of his face and lent intensity to his expression as he crossed the room and took the visitor's chair beside her bed.

Mariah was unable to keep herself from noting the smooth, almost feral grace of his actions. She was equally unable to squelch her body's unexpectedly sharp yearn in his direction when he sat. She wanted to move closer, wanted to lean into his heat and steadying strength. Because she did, and because she knew she didn't dare, she scooted away a few inches instead.

Ever since he'd rescued her in soldier's guise, she'd been unable to go back to thinking of him as the cold, uncaring man she'd thought he was before. If he'd been motivated solely by the needs of his job, he would have tried to capture Lee and Brisbane as they'd chased her from her cabin. Or he could've let them recapture her, waiting until al-Jihad arrived to make his move. Instead, he'd sheltered her with his own body and carried her down the mountain when she'd been unable to walk. And now he was doing everything in his power to keep her safe. Granted, that was part of the job—it was *all* part of the job—but she couldn't help thinking there was something more there, something personal. Something that hummed in the air between them as silence lingered. Some of it was because they didn't dare speak freely, due to all the FBI surveillance equipment, as well as the surveillance they assumed Lee and his terrorist colleagues were using. That meant they were careful to act as though he was nothing more to her than a federal agent assigned to the case. Not the man who'd saved her life, and not a bodyguard awaiting Lee's next move.

That awareness, though, hung heavy between them.

Finally, she broke the quiet to ask, "Do you have more pictures?"

Several times during her hospital stay, he'd brought mug shots of men the FBI thought might be Brisbane, none of which had been a match. Other times, he'd stopped by to see if she needed anything, or to update her on the progress of the investigation. Granted, the latter snippets were undoubtedly doctored to avoid giving away anything to potential listeners, but she still appreciated knowing that her cabin had been released by the crime-scene techs, and that the intelligence community believed that al-Jihad was still out of the country. There had been no word on Lee, though, and the sense of creeping dread that stayed firmly rooted in her stomach made her positive that he was somewhere nearby, watching her.

She shivered involuntarily when Gray handed her a computer printout bearing a dozen photographs, some candids, some mug shots, all of different men with cold, killer's eyes. A jolt of icy fear shot through her when she finally saw the man who had played the curious role of keeping her safe from Lee, while holding her prisoner for some other purpose. She touched his photograph. "That's Brisbane."

"You're sure?"

"Positive."

Gray nodded as though he'd expected the answer, and took the printout from her, but he didn't seem pleased about the break in the case.

"Who is he?" Mariah asked, knowing Gray would only tell her as much as he wanted the terrorists to know.

"He was a guy we know of but don't know much about, a ghost who called himself Felix Smith. He's a midlevel thug we looked at in connection with the Santa Bombings, but didn't pursue. Apparently, that was a mistake." But she sensed that more than just the mistake was bothering him.

"He *was* a ghost?" Mariah pressed. "As in, he's not anymore?"

Gray fixed her with a hard look. "Depends on your definition of *ghost*. His body turned up in a Dumpster this morning." He paused. "Al-Jihad doesn't take failure lightly."

"Oh." A shudder started in her gut and worked its way to her extremities. "Was there…" She faltered, then fell silent.

"There's still no sign of your ex." Though Gray was sitting close to her, he seemed very far away, his expression remote and businesslike.

Mariah pinched the bridge of her nose, trying to force

back an incipient headache. "Is that good news or bad?" Without waiting for him to answer, she continued, "From my perspective it's bad news. If he was dead, I wouldn't have to worry about him coming after me for revenge."

Gray's eyes lost their distance as he zeroed in on her. "You think he'd come after you even if al-Jihad didn't need something from you?"

"I know he would. Lee took the 'till death do us part' thing literally." She paused. "You've seen the letter, right?"

Several weeks after Lee and the others had been incarcerated, she'd picked up her mail from her post office box and found a large manila envelope addressed to her in block print, along with a badly smudged return address and a Denver postmark. Inside had been another envelope, blank. Inside that had been a three-page letter in her ex-husband's elegant script, a cutting missive that could be summarized simply as: "When I get out of here, you're dead. Nobody leaves me." The Feds had tracked the letter as best they could, but the lead had dead-ended quickly. Somehow, Lee had smuggled it out of the ARX Supermax, and another member of the terrorist network had made sure she got it.

Gray's jaw tightened. "Yeah. I've seen it. I wondered whether it was part of something else, though. Word is that your ex is more of a follower than an independent thinker."

"I didn't know that side of him," Mariah said slowly. "The man I married was a golden boy. He was the captain of the football team, class valedictorian, the nice boy my mother always wanted me to meet. He was handsome, charming and persistent, and it seemed to me that he always knew the right thing to say."

"He did," Gray said bluntly. "Someone in al-Jihad's network studied you and drew up a game plan."

"I know." Lee had said as much to her, jeering from the witness stand. She tangled her fingers together and held on tight as she forced herself to continue, "And I fell for it, hook, line and sinker. Pathetic, really."

If Gray had tried to soothe her, she would've shut down. If he'd tried to tell her she wasn't pathetic at all when they both knew that she—or at least her actions back then—had been exactly that, she would've snapped at him. Instead, he sat in silence, watching her with cool gray eyes that she now suspected hid far more emotion than she'd initially given him credit for.

She hesitated, torn. Her inner loner said that the details weren't pertinent to the case, that there was nothing between her and Gray except the investigation. But another, less familiar part of her wanted him to know about her past, wanted him to know *her.* She wasn't sure what she was looking to get back from him—absolution, perhaps? Understanding? Or maybe just a moment of feeling as though she weren't alone in this mess. She, who almost always wanted to be alone.

"My parents were roadies with a heavy-metal band when they met each other," she said, still not entirely sure where the words were coming from, or whether telling him was such a good idea. "My mom was an artist—still is—and my dad was taking some time to 'find himself' after spending nearly a decade getting an advanced degree in structural engineering. He was burned out, she was looking for something more in life… It was love at first sight, and they married and got pregnant within the year. As soon as I was old enough to travel, they went back out onto the road, sometimes crewing for bands, sometimes working carnivals, sometimes just driving their RV from place to place, picking up work where they could and experiencing life to the fullest." She paused. "That was what they called it. Experiencing life."

"What did you call it?"

"It was what I knew. I just called it life." But when he just sat there, looking at her as though he knew that was an evasion, she said, "Okay, maybe I saw the kids who came to the carnivals, how they hung together and knew each other so well, and maybe I wished I could have that." This time her pause was longer, as old resentments banged up against newer guilt. "Sometimes my parents were so wrapped up in each other, there didn't seem to be room for me. They knew I wanted to stay in one place for a while and go to a real school rather than being homeschooled, but that wasn't in their game plan. When they finally did decide to put down roots in Bear Claw, I was applying for college." She lifted a shoulder. "My dorm room was the first place I'd ever stayed for more than a couple of months."

"That must've been a big change," Gray said.

His comment reminded her of something she'd noticed about him before, back during the first two investigations. He didn't ask questions as much as prompt with comments, and then let the silence hang between them until the other person filled the airspace. Before, the tactic had grated on her, making her feel as though he considered himself the maestro, that he had only to gesture and his suspect would tell all. Now, though, it felt different, more personal, as though he wanted to hear her life story. And yeah, he probably did. But was that because he hoped it would give him some new insight into Lee, or because he was interested in her for her own sake? Did he feel the faint hum in the air, the faint tingle of warmth that zinged from him to her and back again?

"You don't want to hear this," she said, going for practical rather than coy. "It has nothing to do with the case."

He tipped his head slightly. "Like it or not, you're part of the case, which makes everything about you relevant. Besides, we're still trying to figure out what Lee and al-Jihad want from you. Any small detail could help."

"I can't imagine you'll learn much hearing about my years of college angst."

"You never know." His voice and expression were impassive, giving away nothing.

From nowhere, sudden frustration bubbled through Mariah. Or maybe it didn't come out of the blue, she realized after a moment of surprise. On some level the irritation had been humming beneath the surface for longer than she'd known, even before Lee had breached the defensive electronic wall around her cabin and taken her hostage. In the months leading up to that, as she'd slowly come awake from the shock of the disaster her life had become, she'd found a kernel of angry impatience growing inside her.

Propelled by that hot irritation, she sat up and faced Gray in her hospital bed, leaning toward him in an effort to make her point, and maybe to see if she could find a crack or two in that cool façade.

"Then what, exactly, do you want to hear?" Her voice rose beyond the sick-sounding whisper she'd been affecting as part of her hospital-bound role, but she didn't care. She'd been lying there, waiting, for nearly two full days; surely Lee would've come for her by now if he were planning on taking her from the hospital. For all they knew, he'd left the country, slipping the noose once again.

That fear, and the knowledge that she wouldn't be safe as long as he was on the loose, sharpened her voice further as she said, "Okay, then. What part of my college angst do you want to hear about? Do you want to know how hard it was to finally be in a position to hang with a group of friends, and realize I didn't want to, that I didn't fit in with the uncool kids, never mind the cool ones? Or maybe how the only way I could really be a part of things was by hiding behind my camera, using it as an excuse to talk to people who forgot me the moment the frame was shot? Oh, wait. I bet you want to know that the reason I moved to New York after I graduated was because I hoped I'd fit in better with an artsy crowd. And how when I got there, when I got my dream job as the lowest of the low in a fashion photog's shop, *that* was when I got to be a part of the cool crowd. That was when I got invited to the clubs, and partied until dawn without the damn camera in my hands."

Gray leaned in and touched one of her hands, where she'd balled it into a fist. "Mariah—"

"I'm not done," she snapped, barreling over him. "Because you probably want to hear about how I met Lee, not in one of those clubs, but in a coffee shop near my apartment. I was sitting at a sidewalk table reading a travel book about Paris—a girl can dream, right?— when someone reaches past me, taps the page I'm on, and a man's voice says, 'I've been there. It's the most beautiful place on earth.' The next thing I know, this absolutely gorgeous guy sits down opposite me and starts telling me about his trip to Paris. Only he doesn't just tell me about himself, he asks me questions, too, and he listens as if he really cared about the answers, like he's really into *me*."

She thumped herself on the chest with one hand, barely registering that the other had somehow become tangled with Gray's, that he'd turned to face her so they were practically knee-to-knee, nose-to-nose.

He drew breath to say something, but she beat him to it, knowing what he was undoubtedly going to remind her. "Of course, I know it was a setup. I didn't back then, though. Back then, I thought it was love at first sight, just like it'd been for my parents." She stared down at her hands, unconsciously tightening her grip on Gray's fingers. "I may not have wanted the child-hood I got, but I wanted what they had. I wanted that connection, the sort of landslide love that swept away everything else and made the rest of the world less im-portant than what the two of them had together." Her voice broke on tears she hadn't even realized were threatening. "I thought I'd found it with Lee. He made me believe in him, in *us,* but it wasn't real. Everything I thought and felt was a lie. Worse, I was so blind, so stupid, that I didn't see him for what he was. You've got to believe me," she said urgently, leaning in closer. "I didn't know. I didn't suspect. If I did, I swear I would've done something before those bombs went off."

And for the first time since three days after the Santa Bombings, when dark-suited men and women had appeared on her doorstep with a search-and-seizure warrant and had asked her to come with them, she thought there might be a chance that the person she was speaking to might finally believe her. She'd lived so long under a cloud of suspicion and self-recrimination that she'd thought she'd never find her way out. But somehow, in that moment, she saw a glimmer of hope, a small clear spot in the dark fog. At its center was a pair of cool eyes.

Gray's face was very close to hers, making her aware of small details she'd been oblivious to before. Fine creases ran from the corners of his mouth and eyes, sug-gesting that he'd once smiled far more than he seemed to now. The touches of silver at his temples made him seem older than his years; she guessed he was in his late thirties. He projected a tough, battle-ready demeanor, but in his eyes, she thought she saw another man—not the soldier or the special agent, but a younger, softer version of both.

"It wasn't your fault, Mariah," he said, gripping both her hands now, as though trying to make her believe.

For a moment she thought he was talking about

whatever had happened to make him the cool, cynical character whose façade he presented to the world. Then, realizing he was talking about Lee, she blushed slightly. Inside her, a coil of uncertainty loosened, even as something else drew tighter. "I lived with him. I was married to him." *He was my first and only lover,* she thought, but didn't say that because that was the one thing she'd never shared with another human being, aside from her ex.

Since Lee hadn't mentioned that fact, either to sneer about it in the courtroom or gloat over it in his letter, she prayed he'd forgotten that detail as inconsequential. But knowing him—or rather knowing the man he'd turned out to be, she feared that he was saving that information for the moment when it would inflict the maximum amount of pain. That was the sort of man he was.

She didn't tell Gray any of that, though. Not because he was a Fed, but because he was holding her hands as though he could keep her safe through that simple contact, and because he was looking at her with a new heat in his eyes, one that sparked something deep inside her, something she thought had died the day she'd learned that Lee had been lying to her from the first moment they'd met.

"He never loved me," she said matter-of-factly, having come to terms with that. "And he'd never been to Paris." It wasn't the most important thing, but it seemed to encapsulate their entire relationship. The first words he'd ever said to her had been a well-researched lie.

Gray's lips twitched. "Bastard."

And though she knew full well that the agent's main purpose in life was bringing down people like Lee, she liked that Gray played along with her in that moment. Incredibly, impossibly, she began to laugh—a deep, belly laugh, tinged with hysteria. Within moments, though, the laughter threatened to turn to sobs as everything started pressing in on her.

It was all too much—the guilt she'd lived with for too long, the fear of captivity, the complications that had arisen in the wake of her escape...once again she was trapped in a life she didn't want, one that kept her from feeling safe and at ease in her own skin.

Face burning from the embarrassment of Gray—of anyone—seeing her on the verge of losing it, she tried to pull away from him. "I'm sorry. You're going to have to give me a moment here."

He didn't leave, though, and he didn't let her withdraw. Instead, he held on to her hands, squeezing tight in support. "Don't beat yourself up," he said. "You didn't ask for any of this."

Tears filming her vision, she shook her head. "But I didn't do anything to stop it."

"You are now."

She blinked, surprised at the intensity in his eyes, and at the warm rush that surged through her at his words, a knife-edge combination of fear and unexpected heat. "I'm scared," she said, the words coming out very small and thin, and shaming her with the weakness they revealed.

"You'd be an idiot not to be." He surprised her, both with the low fervency of his words and by what he did next.

He dropped his head forward so his brow rested on hers. She'd never before thought of him as a man who needed to lean, but in that moment, she felt as though they were propping each other up.

"Gray?" she said, the single word a question that encompassed all the thoughts suddenly jammed inside her head. *What's going on?* she wanted to ask, *Do you feel it, too?* But she didn't have the guts, had never had the guts to do what mattered.

"I'll protect you," he said, the three words punching through her in a heartfelt vow, because she instinctively knew he wasn't just promising to protect a witness, or potential asset. He was promising to protect *her.*

"I know you will," she said, trying not to make more of this than it really was. He was tired; they both were. The situation had thrown them together, and it had broken down barriers that perhaps would've been better left in place. Trying to resurrect some of those barriers, she said, "Because it's your job."

"And because of this," he replied. Then he tipped his face up, and touched his lips to hers.

## Chapter Five

Mariah froze as heat raced through her veins and an unexpected flare of connection threatened to unlock a
torrent of wants and needs too long denied. Her rational
brain screamed that there was a cop at the door, and
though Gray was the only one watching the in-room
surveillance, everything was undoubtedly being caught
on tape. More, experience had taught her that desire
could make her do very stupid things.

But as his mouth slanted against hers and his lips
exerted subtle suction, teasing hers apart for a touch
of tongue, a nip of teeth, she couldn't find the strength
to pull away.

She hadn't expected him to kiss her. Or at least not
now, not under these circumstances. It seemed out of
character for a man like Gray, who might push the
boundaries of his position and his boss, but was
always aware of himself, always on the job. Yet at the
same time she could understand it, had felt—and
denied—the chemistry from that first moment they'd
met during her initial interrogations, and again when

he'd rescued her from the cabin and shielded her with his own body.

Now, realizing from the urgent press of his lips that he felt the same sharp, greedy attraction, she leaned into him, opened to him. And if a piece of her wondered whether this was another layer of manipulation, she told herself to enjoy now, analyze later.

He groaned when her tongue touched his, a harsh rattle at the back of his throat, and he held himself tense for a moment, as though fighting the mad impulse that had roared up and was riding them both, spurring them on. Mariah knew she should pull away, knew they both should, but she couldn't make herself break their partial embrace any more than she could force herself to assess his motives.

Gray's lips were clever and agile, and far softer than she would have expected, based on what she knew of the man. His skin was cool to the touch, which was definitely what she would've expected, but it heated rapidly, bringing an unfamiliar sizzle of feminine power surging through Mariah.

Going with that power, which made her feel as though she were in control, in charge, she changed the angle of the kiss and added a light scrape of teeth, then feathered a breath along his jaw, and into the soft place behind his ear, where she herself was supersensitive.

His breath caught on a second groan and he shuddered against her, then retaliated, dragging his lips across her throat, taking her earlobe between his teeth and biting down gently.

Mariah angled her head, baring herself to the sensuous torture and moaning when he obliged. Then his lips returned to hers and she gave herself over to the kiss, losing her edge of control in the heat that rose up to surround them, consume them. She was vaguely conscious that she'd shifted, uncrossing her legs and leaning back as he stood and followed her down, so they were almost—but not quite—wrapped together on the narrow hospital bed. Still, though, their fingers were tangled together, a last hold on sanity.

Wanting to touch the big, masculine body that rose above her, she released his hands at the same moment he let go of hers. They reached for each other. Touched each other. And froze.

Reality returned with a cold, hard slap that did little to temper the burning heat rocketing through Mariah's body. What the hell was she doing? What was she thinking?

She eased away from him and he from her, so their lips were no longer touching. Still, they were wrapped in an almost-embrace, with her palms pressed flat against the hard planes of his chest, and his hands cupping her waist in a caress that had perhaps been intended to help soothe away the danger and complications that had brought them together in the first place.

It was precisely those issues that rose up now, and had Mariah saying, "Bad idea."

She could feel the hammer of his heart beneath her palms, and hear passion in the rasp of his breath. A mad part of her wanted him to argue, wanted him to take the decision away from her, simply wanted him to *take* her, there on the hospital bed, with a cop standing guard just outside the swinging door and the video cameras taping away. The daringness of it surged through her bloodstream, a heady mix of heat and temptation. But instead of moving in to kiss away her reservations, Gray released her and stood up, stood back, his color draining.

Feeling exposed, though she was wearing yoga pants and a T-shirt, Mariah sat up and drew the thin hospital sheet around her waist. She focused on those small tasks, giving them both a moment to recover. But when she glanced back at Gray, she found that he still stood there, looking shell-shocked.

Then she saw him retreat behind his cool agent's façade; she could all but see the shields slam down, separating her from what little emotion he'd allowed to leak out during the kiss. When he spoke, his voice grated. "That can't happen again."

Mariah buried a small slice of hurt and nodded. "You were comforting me, and it got out of hand. That's not a federal crime."

"Got out of hand is an understatement." He grimaced, raking a hand through his brown hair, mussing it. The result made him look younger, like the man she'd thought she'd seen just before their kiss. His eyes, though, were hard and uncompromising, very much those of the soldier, or the special agent. "Look," he said, seeming to make an effort to soften his tone, "this isn't going to work. I'll deal with the tapes of the last few minutes' worth of surveillance, then find someone else to take over this part of the case."

"You're quitting?" The thought brought a clutch of fear. She hated the idea of losing the one person she'd considered even partially an ally. And that, she realized, had been a mistake. Gray wasn't her friend or her ally, and he certainly wasn't going to be her lover. When had she lost track of that? How had she let herself be so foolish based on a spark of chemistry and the fact that he'd rescued her?

"It'll be safer for you if the agent protecting you isn't emotionally involved in the case."

She felt a shimmer of warmth at that, but squelched it and said, "We can agree to keep our distance from each other." She would've reached out to him, but didn't dare touch him, not with the residual hum of their kisses still speeding through her bloodstream. So, instead, she curled her fingers into the hospital sheet, trying not to let his answer matter. "Please don't leave because of what just happened." There was a faint tremor in her voice, warning that her emotions were suddenly too close to the surface when she'd successfully kept them buried for so long.

"I'm not leaving because of what just happened, or at least not the way I think you mean." He paused, and in his eyes she thought she saw a flash of regret. But there was none of that in his voice, which went cool and remote, very much that of Special Agent Grayson when he said, "The emotions I was talking about, the ones that don't have any place in an official investigation…they don't have anything to do with you, or what just happened."

*Ouch. That was direct,* she thought. But even so, it took a moment before she got it. When she did, she sucked in a quiet breath and let it out again on a slow sound of pain. "You lost someone in the bombings."

She didn't need his slow nod of confirmation to know she had it right. It explained so many things, from his cold, almost brutal demeanor during the first investigation and his insistence on being involved in the jailbreak case, to his disobeying orders to sneak up and spy on her cabin for no other reason than because he suspected that she might still be involved with Lee.

"So you'll understand why you'd be better off with someone else," he said, his expression implacable.

"No, actually, I don't," she said, fighting to keep her voice level, and conscious of the others who might be listening. "We both want the same thing. We both want Lee, al-Jihad and everyone associated with them either dead or behind bars, right? There's no difference."

"There's one very important difference." Gray surprised her by moving into her space again, and leaning down so she could feel the heat of him.

"Oh?" she said, damning herself for the weakness of her voice, which had gone nearly to a husky whisper. "What would that be?"

"You want your ex off the streets so you'll be safe. I just want him off the streets." His eyes bored into hers. In case she'd missed his message, he spelled it out: "In the second scenario, you're expendable."

"Yet you kissed me." It wasn't the most important point, perhaps, but it was the one she wanted out there.

"It shouldn't have happened. Chemistry can make us imagine things that aren't real. It can complicate things that shouldn't be complicated."

*But all of this is complicated!* she wanted to snap at him, but didn't, because she saw a flicker of something in his expression—a hint of wariness, maybe, or a crack in his armor.

She wanted to lean in and touch her lips to his, and see if she could turn the crack into a split, and get him to tell her what was really going on inside his head. But who was she to presume to know what a man was thinking? Maybe it was exactly as he'd said. Maybe she was a means to an end—nothing more—and the kiss had been, just as they'd both said, a mistake.

So instead of leaning in, she stayed put. "Please reconsider, Gray. I don't trust Johnson to do the right thing."

He didn't argue that point. He did, however, straighten and move away, saying over his shoulder, "I'll take care of it. It's the least I can do."

He pushed through the door and was gone before she could ask what he meant by that. Did he mean he owed her because he'd rescued her, and therefore felt partially responsible for her safety? Was it because he and his coworkers hadn't yet brought the escapees to justice? Or, in the end, was it because of the kiss?

Mariah touched her lips, feeling the phantom press of his mouth against hers. "Leave it," she whispered, trying not to dwell on what had just happened, and what it had made her feel, a response that had been so much stronger than she'd expected or wanted. But unexpectedly, the words brought a new urge, strong and fierce. *Leave it.* She should just go, take off, disappear someplace where neither Lee nor the Feds could find her.

The thought was so liberating, the desire so strong, that she was on her feet before she was even aware of having moved. She was halfway across the room when the door swung open again. She looked up, her heart kicking at the thought that Gray had come back to argue some more, or maybe apologize, though he didn't seem like the sort of man to apologize for telling the truth, hurtful or not.

It wasn't Gray, though. It was a uniformed officer, presumably the one who'd been guarding her out in the hallway.

He blocked the door and avoided her eyes, making her wonder how much of her and Gray's exchange he'd heard, and what else Gray had told him. But the cop said only, "Special Agent Grayson said I should guard you eyes-on until he gets back with his replacement."

"Oh," she said faintly. "I was just…" She trailed off. "Never mind."

She got back in bed and lay on her side, facing away from the officer, who ducked through the door to pull his chair inside the room. She knew it was rude of her to all but ignore him, knew she'd feel bad about that later, but she didn't care right then. She was tired, sad and hurting, and just wanted to be left alone with the realization that Gray hadn't agreed to protect her because of the attraction that snapped between them or because he was a good guy at heart. He'd agreed to the plan because, like his boss, he'd seen the value in using her. She'd been right—the kiss had been another layer of manipulation, though seemingly not a calculated one. There had been nothing personal about it at all. Worse, the cop inside the room was proof positive that Gray didn't trust her one bit.

*Which is fine,* she told herself. *Because I don't trust him, either.* They'd moved from what she'd thought was the beginning of a truce that might've become more, to…nothing. He was gone and she had a feeling that he wasn't coming back.

More important, she wasn't sure she wanted him to.

WITH MARIAH SAFELY GUARDED by the officer on duty, Gray found an empty room down the hall and snagged a landline to dial out. When the phone rang for the fourth time on the other end, he started cursing under his breath. "Come on, come on. Pick up."

The line clicked live, and a familiar voice said, "Jonah Fairfax here."

"It's Gray. I need your help."

"Anything," the other agent said without a moment's hesitation. "What can I do?"

It still surprised Gray how quickly the two of them had become allies, especially given that the first time they'd met, Gray had arrested Fax none too gently. Granted, at the time Gray had not known that Fax was undercover, and that the prison break had been a setup. Fax had gone into the ARX Supermax Prison under-cover on the orders of his boss, Jane Doe, and hadn't realized that she'd turned and was working for al-Jihad until too late—after the jailbreak and subsequent chaos. He'd managed to avoid totally compromising the mission by hooking up with Bear Claw Medical Exam-iner Chelsea Swan and several of her friends. The small group, which had included a few trusted members of the FBI and the Bear Claw PD, had averted a disaster and captured one of the escaped convicts, al-Jihad's closest lieutenant, Muhammad Feyd.

In the aftermath, Fax and Chelsea had paired up and eventually gotten engaged, though they had put off the wedding until Chelsea was finished with her FBI training. She'd pursued FBI training as part of a long-delayed dream. Until then, Fax was committed to chasing down al-Jihad and the others, while doing his bit for the wedding plans—which, he'd admitted to Gray privately, had so far consisted mostly of staying out of Chelsea's way. Gray had nodded and tried to grin, but as with the subject of holidays, the topic of weddings and marriages made him cringe.

He and Fax might have met as adversaries, but in the months since then they'd become cautious and somewhat unlikely friends, drawn together because both of them were viewed with serious suspicion by the bulk of the local and federal law-enforcement professionals. Fax was distrusted because no matter how much evidence proved that he'd been acting on orders, the fact remained that he'd helped al-Jihad and the others escape from prison. Heck, even Gray would've probably mistrusted the other agent, if he himself hadn't come under a similar cloud of suspicion not long after he'd arrested Fax. Back then, when Johnson had accused him of colluding with al-Jihad, Gray's only and best defense had been to blame his personal problems for the choices he'd made, when, in reality, he'd gone with his gut and had been wrong.

Well, after what had just happened with Mariah, his gut was 0-for-2. He'd thought he could use her without letting things get complicated. He'd been dead wrong.

"From your utter silence, I'm guessing that whatever's going on, it's complicated," Fax said. "Are you in the hospital?"

"Yeah. Why?"

"I just hit the parking lot, and I'm about to get in the elevator. See you in a couple of minutes." Fax hung up.

At least something was going his way, Gray thought. If Fax was already there, he could take over Mariah's protection immediately. That'd be better for everyone involved. And if the decision kindled an acid burn in Gray's gut, nobody else needed to know about it.

Gray was standing by the elevators when Fax stepped out. Just shy of six feet, with close-clipped black hair, hard blue eyes and the faint thread of a scar running through one dark eyebrow, the other agent was a tough, no-nonsense scrapper from a police family, not unlike Gray's own. Fax kept his own counsel, went outside the box when the situation called for it and had only one vulnerability Gray was aware of—namely Chelsea.

Fax was one of the few men Gray would trust at his back in a firefight, which made him the man for this particular job, too. And if a small voice at the back of Gray's head pointed out that he'd just put Mariah's safety on a par with his own, when he'd been so careful to tell her that wasn't the case, then he ignored it just as he'd ignored the sense of disquiet that had poked at him when he'd put the cop in her room and abandoned his surveillance post. Those were gut-level twinges, and his gut had been less than reliable of late.

Fax nodded in greeting. "Hey. What's up?"

"Any news?" Gray asked, though he had little hope

that the case had broken in the thirty minutes since his last update.

"More of the same," Fax replied. "There's a good chance that al-Jihad is out of the country, and there's been no word on Mawadi, Jane Doe or the others. The Bear Claw PD's Internal Affairs Department is taking a look at the local cops, trying to figure out whether there's an in-house conspirator, and, if so, who it might be. The investigation's being led by Romo Sampson. Career cop, has the reputation of being a hard-ass, but usually he calls it right. At the moment, he's looking long and hard at the coroner's office. I guess the head coroner has both friends and enemies in high places, and she and Romo have a past."

"None of which gets us any closer to Mawadi," Gray said, frustration riding him hard. Aware that they were exposed even with the normal hospital bustle swirling around them, Gray moved them into a nearby alcove and kept his voice pitched low. "I need you to take over the protection detail. I've got to get out of here."

Fax's scarred eyebrow rose, but he said only, "You've got another angle to work?"

If he said yes, Fax would accept that without further explanation, Gray knew. But it would be a lie. Shaking his head he said, "I've got to get out of here. This assignment's making me crazy."

"The assignment or the woman?"

Gray shot his friend a quick look. "Why? What have you heard?"

"Nothing. I saw the two of you together in the interview tapes, and again the other day when you pulled her down off the ridgeline. From the way you were acting with each other, I thought there might be something going on. Sparks, at the very least."

Scowling, Gray muttered, "I think all that wedding planning has fried your brain. She and I weren't sparking, we were arguing."

Fax snorted. "Whatever. Are you trying to tell me it's my imagination?"

Gray started to…and then exhaled on a curse, scrubbing both hands across his face in a vain effort to relieve some of the tension—and wipe away the memory of a very big mistake that had felt like something else entirely. "I kissed her. Just now, in her room, under the damn surveillance cameras. We were fighting over something—I don't even remember what. One second we were going at it, and then we were…" He trailed off.

"Going at it?" Fax offered, looking devilishly amused.

"You're not helping." Gray shook his head. "Anybody could've come in gunning for her, and I would've been beyond useless. What kind of an agent does something like that?"

Fax shot him a level look. "This one, for starters. Been there, done that, bought the diamond ring. Not that I'm advocating that method of courtship, but if you're looking for someone to warn you off, you've come to the wrong guy."

"I'm. Not. Courting." Realizing he was clenching his jaw hard enough to crack a molar, Gray consciously relaxed his suddenly strung-tight body. "And if I were,

Mariah wouldn't be where I'd be headed. She's closed-off, short-tempered and stubborn as an ox."

"So are you," Fax retorted. "And I don't think too many oxen look like her. Then again, I'm a city boy. What do I know?"

Gray glared because Fax knew damn well he was another city boy, straight from the rough side of Chicago. Yeah, maybe he was the first in his cop family to go to a big college out of state, the first to take the plunge and go federal, but still. Even city boys knew it worked best to keep policework in the family. Cops understood other cops. People on the outside—people like photographers, or whatever Mariah would be when this was all over—didn't understand the life, didn't grasp the dangers and demands. His ex-wife, Stacy, had come from a cop family, and even her familiarity with the demands of policework hadn't been enough to overcome the difficulties created by his job.

That, and the fact that they might've had lust going for them, but when the sex had mellowed, they had belatedly realized they didn't have a damn thing in common.

"None of it matters right now," Gray said, as much to himself as to Fax. "I'm out. I'm done. I want you to take over the surveillance detail while I do what needs to be done." The frustrated anger inside him needed an outlet. He was stirred up, churned up, and he wasn't going to do anybody any good in that state. And when it came right down to it, he was tired of playing by the rules. Forget due process—he was looking for results.

This time, he was damn well turning in his resignation and making it stick.

Fax took a good long look at him, then shook his head. "All indications say that al-Jihad's not even in the country anymore."

"Maybe not. But Mawadi is." And if Gray's need to hunt the bastard had suddenly become far stronger than before, and far more personal, nobody but him needed to know it.

"If we can't find him," Fax said, meaning the FBI, "then how do you expect to?" He shot Gray a sidelong look. "If you're serious about this, I'd think you'd be looking to use the woman, not leave her behind."

Gray growled, but Fax had a point. He was being inconsistent and reactive, neither of which were good traits when it came to doing the job. But that was exactly why he needed to get away from the hospital, away from Mariah. She was stirring him up, distracting him. When he was near her, he wasn't focused on the case—he was thinking about her, looking at her. Wondering how she would feel against him, how she would taste on his lips.

Now that he knew, it would only be worse, because he couldn't pursue the attraction without risking her safety and the vow he'd made on a tiny grave.

"The dead deserve my full attention," he finally said. "And Mariah needs a bodyguard who's protecting her, not climbing all over her."

"The dead are gone," Fax said quietly. "You're not." He held up a hand to forestall Gray's knee-jerk response. "That's not to say the dead don't deserve justice—of course they do. But their being dead doesn't mean that you don't get to have a life."

"She's not what I want," Gray said starkly, though there was so much more to it than that.

Fax looked at him for a long moment before he nodded slowly. "Okay, then. I'll watch out for her. You want to introduce me? The changeover might come easier from you."

"I doubt it," Gray said, largely because he was too tempted to see her one last time. "You go ahead. She'll understand."

"If you're sure." Fax stuck out his hand. "I'll keep her alive. You keep yourself alive. Deal?"

"Deal." Gray was reaching to shake when all hell broke loose.

## Chapter Six

Gray was sprinting for the source of the alarmed cries—Mariah's room—before he was even aware of having moved. Fax pounded at his heels. The hospital staffers' shouts of "Where is she?" and "She was there a minute ago!" warned him that they were already too late.

A uniformed cop stood in the doorway, wild-eyed. It wasn't the officer who'd been on duty when Gray had left her, maybe five minutes earlier, which was a very bad sign. When the cop saw Gray, he snapped, "What the hell happened?"

Gray didn't answer. He pushed past the cop into Mariah's hospital room, expecting to see signs of a struggle, and the officer on duty injured, maybe down for good. Instead, he found the room nearly pristine. The bed was badly rumpled, though he suspected he was at least part of the cause of that—and the memory brought a kick of heat and anger. He was furious at himself for letting emotion override duty. He'd been sulking in the hallway when he should've been in the surveillance room, doing his damn job.

Which was exactly why he'd wanted Fax to take over, because his growing attraction to Mariah was distracting him, churning him up and causing him to make mistakes, perhaps even fatal ones. But the heat eating at him didn't emerge as rage; it turned to ice. He felt the change, felt himself closing off and going killer-cold.

"Call it in and seal the room," he said to the cop, then spun away, gesturing for Fax to follow as he jogged to the surveillance room. "Come on. The bastard is bound to be on tape. That'll give us a starting point, and information."

They would see whether the cop had taken her, or been taken along with her, and where they'd gone. The tapes would tell Gray where to start looking, and what he was looking for. That was the upside of being part of a well-stocked organization like the FBI.

Gray and Fax grabbed chairs, and Gray started running back the tapes, first taking a few precious seconds to erase the part where he had kissed Mariah and then working forward, moving as fast as he could, knowing every second counted.

Gray scanned the film, muttering curses under his breath as his blood beat with the need to find her. Mariah was his. Or rather, he corrected himself, she was *his responsibility*. And if she suffered—or worse, died—because he'd fouled up, then it would be on his soul. Again.

MARIAH AWOKE IN DARKNESS, swathed mummylike in sheets and gagged with a towel jammed in her mouth. She fought to struggle but could barely move; she was strapped down to something hard and flat, bound by restricting strips that crossed her chest, waist and ankles.

Panic seized her, as she felt the vertigo of motion and heard the growl of engine noise. She inhaled to scream, and nearly choked on the heavy, chemical smell suffusing the air around her. The fumes had her nasal passages closing, making her gag and fight for breath. When lack of oxygen made her even more terrified, threatening to send her over the edge, she told herself to calm down, to think. Focus.

It wasn't easy, but she managed it. Her heart still hammered and tears leaked from the corners of her eyes, but she slowed her breathing through sheer force of will. She could get enough air—barely—through her nostrils, and suck some through the towel. She wouldn't suffocate, at least not immediately. But that was small comfort as she began to suspect that she was bound to a backboard and zipped inside a coroner's body bag. She could feel the heavy plastic with the tips of her fingers, and it stood to reason. Lee and the others had escaped from the ARX Supermax in body bags, on gurneys transported out of the jail in a coroner's van. If she had to guess, from the tip and sway as the vehicle transporting her rounded a corner, that was exactly what had been done with her as well.

It fit with Lee's twisted sense of irony. Knowing him, she was probably lying in the very body bag he planned to use to dispose of her when the time came.

Revulsion tore at her, alongside despair, but she fought both with the hard practicality she'd been forced to learn over the past two years. If she vomited with a gag in her mouth, she'd aspirate and die. If she despaired and gave up, then Lee had already won, and that wasn't acceptable. Over the past few months, as she'd reawakened to herself as a person, she'd begun to see beauty once again in the dawn and dusk, and the woods around her home. She'd discovered a new sense of purpose, of determination. And she'd kissed a man and felt the burn of lust. Maybe he hadn't been the right man, maybe it hadn't been the right time, but the kiss had proved that she was able to respond sexually. She'd worried now and then, late at night when her brain insisted on replaying hurtful segments of her marriage, that that capability had died. She was still alive, dammit. Kissing Gray had proved that, if nothing else.

The burn of remembered heat hardened her resolve. She wasn't giving up without a fight. Not this time. But what could she do from where she was? She was trapped. Helpless.

Panic washed through her at the thought, but she forced it away, made herself think and remember what had happened, how she'd gotten where she'd wound up.

*The cop,* she thought, remembering that she'd rolled onto her side so the officer sitting just inside the door couldn't see her tears, which had been mostly out of frustration and anger, and a bit of self-pity following Gray's precipitous exit.

Her eyes filmed again, and a desperate wish shimmered through her. *Please find me,* she thought, as though her brain waves could magically reach inside his thick skull. *I don't care how you feel about me, or whether you walk away afterwards, as long as you get me out of this before Lee does…whatever he's going to do.*

The thought brought a shudder of dread, one that threatened to undermine her sense of purpose. But she fought not to give in to the terror.

*Lee needs something from me,* she reminded herself, trying to breathe through the panic. *Otherwise, I'd already be dead.* But how long would that logic hold? At what point would the terrorists decide that keeping her alive was too much of an effort and just kill her?

As if answering her question, the driver swerved, hit the brakes and brought the vehicle to a skidding halt. Inertia made Mariah's insides slosh sickeningly, but the flat surface beneath her didn't move, except to give a metallic rattle, adding weight to her suspicion that she was strapped to a gurney that'd been locked into place in a coroner's van. Lee would've liked the convenience, as well as the psychological torture, of her waking up inside her own shroud.

*Bastard,* Mariah thought, fanning the anger and hatred because both were better than fear.

Then she heard muffled footsteps approaching the rear of the vehicle, and the fear took over. She whimpered involuntarily behind the gag, hoping against hope that the footsteps belonged to a savior but knowing deep down inside that they didn't.

The door locks popped and she heard a door open. A man's voice asked, "Did anyone see you take her?"

It was Lee.

Sick dread rolled through Mariah in waves at the sound of her ex's too-familiar tones, draining her resolve in an instant.

"No." The second voice, coming from very close

to her, was thick with emotion. She thought it was the cop from her room and became sure of it when he said, "I did what I was told. You said you'd tell me where my wife—"

"Help me switch her to the other car," Lee interrupted. "Someone will call and tell you where to find your family."

That explained the abduction, Mariah thought, her heart clutching for the cop. The terrorists had gotten to the officer, using the best leverage of all. Family.

A slice of despair suddenly surfaced as Mariah inwardly acknowledged that she might never see her parents again, that she should have tried to fix that relationship when she'd had the chance. She hadn't understood why they'd needed to move away any more than they'd understood why she needed to stay. That, combined with Mariah's awful guilt over knowing she'd brought Lee into their lives only to have him destroy her father's career and self-respect, had driven a wedge into their already estranged family unit.

She should've apologized a thousand times over, should've done more to help them start over. Instead, she'd walled herself away in her isolated cabin.

Mariah felt sick, then even sicker still when the men climbed into the back of the van with her. The vehicle shuddered under their weight. Moments later, she felt the men approach her and pause. She held herself still, trapped and terrified.

An unzipping noise reverberated through the dark space that enclosed her, and suddenly there was light again, she could see again. But that wasn't a relief, because what she saw was Lee's face as he bent over her, wrinkling his nose at the smell coming from the bag's lining. His beautiful blue eyes were lit with unholy satisfaction and excitement.

"Hello, Mariah," he said, his voice sounding as cultured and urbane as ever, his whole demeanor giving no evidence that he was talking to a woman bound in a body bag. "This shouldn't take long at all. A short drive, a little session with al-Jihad where you'll tell us what we want to know, and after that…well, we'll see what happens after that, won't we, sweetheart?"

The Feds had said Lee was a follower, with the undercover agent, Fairfax, even going as far as to call him a lemming, a weak personality who chased the leader. But they didn't know him the way Mariah did. When it came to his wife—or the woman he perceived as still being his wife despite the paperwork that said otherwise—Lee was no follower. He went his own way, and didn't give a damn what anyone else said, least of all her.

She'd married him thinking she was in love. But she'd found herself in hell. And now he was going to do everything in his power to put her right back there, or worse.

Heart pounding with fear and rage, Mariah narrowed her eyes, not caring that tears leaked from their corners as she screamed against her gag, telling him how much she hated him, and that she wasn't afraid of him, not anymore. She struggled against the straps, wanting to rake her nails across his lying face, needing to do something, anything, to prove that she wasn't the doormat she'd become while she was married to him.

He smiled and leaned in to kiss her cheek, though she struggled and turned her face away. "I missed you, too. This time I'll be very certain not to let you get away from me. We can't have the others thinking I'm unable to control my wife, can we?"

Refusing to look at him anymore, Mariah focused on the second man. The cop stood nearby, tense and unhappy, and coated in the stink of fear. His eyes were unfocused, turned inward, as though he were picturing what the terrorists were doing to his family.

Mariah could relate, but she felt no sympathy. She felt only anger. *How could you?* she wanted to shout at him. *You're one of the good guys!*

Then, in the distance, she heard the rattle of an engine being driven too hard, too fast. Fear seized her. Was it al-Jihad?

But Lee jolted and cursed at the sound, suggesting that the other car was unexpected. "Come on. Let's get her transferred to the minivan."

The cop obeyed, but his expression didn't change; it was as though he were acting on autopilot, beyond himself with fear and shock.

The two men unlatched the gurney and started muscling it off the van, but had difficulty with the folding legs in their haste. Mariah's pulse pounded and her thoughts raced as the surface she was bound to lurched this way and that. She saw forest on either side of her, and caught a glimpse of a brown sign that told her she was somewhere within Bear Claw Canyon State Park. The park, which covered thousands of wilderness acres, offered a steady stream of tourist income, along with the perfect hiding place for nefarious deeds, ranging from teenagers sneaking time alone, to drug deals and even murder and body dumps.

That was what Lee and the others had used it for the day they had escaped from prison, disposing of the bodies of four slain guards and an assistant coroner in a small cave off the main drag. Mariah whimpered at the back of her throat, wondering if this was the same place.

Once they had the gurney off the van, they started hustling it toward a second vehicle, this one a minivan with its back deck wide open and the engine running. Another figure was visible in the driver's seat, though Mariah saw him only briefly as the men approached the minivan.

"Hurry up, damn it," Lee snapped. "If you don't help me get the bitch out of here, your family's dead."

"They're already dead, aren't they?" the cop asked in a dull monotone, his face hardening from shock and grief to a mask of rage.

"Of course not. They're fine." But Lee's answer was too quick, and his eyes showed the lie.

Cursing, the cop exploded into action, shoving the gurney straight into Lee, trapping him against the minivan's back deck. Lee swore as the gurney yawed in his grasp, threatening to tip over.

Surprise and vertigo seized Mariah for a second before she saw her chance to escape. Once she saw it, though, she grabbed on to it, knowing it might be the only shot at freedom she had. Shouting inwardly, she threw her weight in the direction in which she was tipping, hoping against hope that would be enough.

It was. Lee yelled profanities as the gurney flipped and Mariah plummeted to the ground.

She landed hard, banging her head and exhaling in a rush when the metal gurney came down with its full weight on top of her. It took her a second to realize that the jolt had popped the strap securing her arms. She was partway free!

Struggling to breathe through her gag, she tried to free herself from the confines of the body bag. She was in darkness again, having fallen face forward, but she managed to roll onto her side. Working quickly, sobbing with fear, she ripped open the bag, then yanked at the strap binding her chest. Almost clear!

Lee was shouting. She heard him curse, and heard another man's voice join in, followed by the sound of running footsteps and the cry of, "The cop's taking off. *Shoot him!*"

Mariah screamed behind her gag when gunfire cracked above her, three times in quick succession. She didn't know if the cop had run in order to escape, to draw the attention of the incoming vehicle, which sounded as though it were nearly on top of them, or to buy her time to get free of her bonds, but she'd take the distraction no matter what the reason. She yanked the towel out of her mouth, tearing her parched lips in the process but not caring about the pain because it meant she could finally breathe.

Sucking in deep, wrenching breaths and sobbing in relief, she reached for her ankles, which were strapped to each other, but not attached to the backboard she'd been secured to. Before she could get to them, though, the gurney was lifted off her and Lee rasped, "You're not going anywhere without me."

He shifted his gun to his other hand and reached down to grab her. Screaming, she struck back, fisting her hands together and swinging them at his face. The blow was a solid connection that reverberated up her arm and sent Lee reeling back, roaring obscenities through split and bleeding lips. Fury lit his eyes as he switched the gun to his dominant hand and leveled it at her. "You're going to regret that, *wife*."

The man still in the minivan lurched halfway out, snapping something that, even in a foreign language, sounded like, "We're leaving, *now!*"

Lee's finger tightened on the trigger. Mariah thought it was over. She was dead.

Then gunfire split the air, but it came from the tree line, not Lee's gun. Bullets glanced off the minivan, one shattering the back window. The driver shouted, leaped back into the minivan and hit the gas. Lee dove in the open back deck, yelling, "Go, go, go!"

The vehicle peeled out, spraying Mariah with sand and debris, but she didn't protect herself. She was staring slack-jawed in shock as Gray burst from the tree line, running flat-out after the minivan.

She screamed, "Gray, no!" but he didn't hear her. Or if he heard her, he paid no heed.

He flung himself through the open back deck, tackling Lee and hammering a punch into her ex's jaw as the vehicle flew down a dirt access road and disappeared.

A scant second later, four official vehicles burst from the tree line in the direction Gray had come from. Two skidded to a stop near Mariah and the hospital van. The other two raced in pursuit of the minivan.

"Are you okay?" The cop was back, fresh grief and remorse in his eyes. "I flagged them down, but—"

"Don't say anything more," said a big, brown-haired man as he emerged from one of the official vehicles. He had wide-palmed hands, uncompromising features and a local PD badge. "As your friendly local Internal Affairs stiff, I'm advising you to shut the hell up now." He cuffed the cop, who went with him, unresisting.

Mariah simply stared, uncomprehending, as too many things happened around her at once, seemingly unconnected in her brain. Time passed in a fog…yet there was no sign of Gray. The chase cars hadn't come back, and for all the agents and cops piling out of the two big black SUVs and the cruisers pulling up behind them, not a single radio relayed news of Gray's safe return.

"Hey." A man squatted down in front of her and held out a hand. "Can I help you up?"

He had black hair and dark blue eyes, and he looked familiar, though Mariah didn't think they'd been officially introduced. "You're Fairfax."

"That's right. I'm also Gray's friend." Moving slowly, as though he were afraid she would panic if he went too quickly, he eased her feet out of the body bag and undid the straps that were the last things holding her down.

Still, though, even once she was free, she couldn't seem to stand. She just stared up at Fairfax. "Where is he?"

Gray had come for her. The realization shimmered through her. Whether or not he wanted her, or wanted to want her, he'd come for her. He'd chased Lee, had been fighting him as the car disappeared. Then the gunshots. What had happened? Was he alive? Dead?

"We're working on that. Come on. Let's get you out of there." Fairfax hauled her to her feet. He used the bulk of his own body to block her view of the scene, but she caught sight of the corner of the gurney and the still-idling van, and shuddered.

If Lee hadn't arranged to transfer her to the second vehicle…if Gray and the others hadn't figured out where they would be…

Frowning, she glanced at Gray's friend. "How did you find me?"

"GPS." The agent nodded back at the van. "Hospital property."

Mariah shuddered. "Lucky me."

"Maybe not." Fairfax sounded seriously grim. "Especially when you consider that they knew to disable the transponder on the prison van they stole during the jailbreak."

She wrapped her arms around herself as the sharp air cut through her yoga pants and thin T-shirt, and she became aware of the cold ground beneath her sock-clad feet. "Maybe Lee forgot."

"Maybe. Or maybe this was meant as a distraction. Maybe we were supposed to chase the van out here and find it abandoned, while other members of the cell do something else. But what?" Fairfax glanced down, seeming to notice for the first time that she was shivering against him. "Sorry. I'm thinking out loud. Let's get you into a squad car."

But before they'd gone two steps, the big black chase

cars reappeared through the trees. Mariah stopped dead, almost afraid to hope. Then the rear door of the first SUV swung open and Gray emerged, looking bruised and battered, with one suit coat sleeve torn most of the way off and scratches along the side of his face. But he was alive. He was up and moving.

He straightened and scanned the crowd, and his eyes locked on her.

Mariah's heart jolted, then started pounding in her ears as he strode toward her, looking simultaneously furious and implacable, and very much like the soldier who had saved her life twice now, once up on the mountain and again just now. When he reached her, he stopped a few feet away, and flicked a glance at Fairfax.

"I'll take her," Gray said, and he exchanged a look with his friend that conveyed a great deal more than those three small words.

Mariah knew she should be offended by the idea of being passed from one man to the next. And she would be, as soon as she stopped shaking. "Did you get him?" she asked, her voice barely above a whisper.

Gray shook his head. "Bastard booted me out of the minivan. Chase car nearly ran me over before I rolled into some scrub." Before Mariah could react to that— if she could even figure out how—he raked her from head to toe with a cool-eyed inspection. But there was heat in his voice when he said, "Are you okay?"

*I am now,* she meant to say, just as she meant to hold it together and be the practical, no-nonsense woman she prided herself on being these days.

Instead, she shook her head as tears filmed her vision.

"I hate this," she whispered. "I hate all of it." She meant the fear and the danger, and maybe—even a little bit— she meant him, and the emotions he stirred in her, emotions she couldn't deal with. Not now. Maybe not ever.

"I know," he said gruffly. "I'm sorry." And again, the few words he spoke were loaded with meaning. He approached her, and Fairfax stepped away, leaving the two of them to face each other.

Gray would've held her if she'd wanted it; she could see it in his eyes. He would've let her pretend that the embrace meant as much to him as it did to her. But he'd made his position crystal clear back at the hospital— he wasn't in this for her, and he didn't intend to let their connection interfere with his priority, which was bringing the bombers to justice. Well, she told herself, that was just fine with her, because she wouldn't be safe until Lee and the others were off the street. Gray wanted nothing but business between them? Fine, that was what she'd give him. And, frankly, the sooner he and the others did their jobs and she was free to go back to rebuilding her life, the better.

So she leaned away from him and said, "What now?"

He looked at her long and hard, and after a moment his expression went cool and took on an edge she hadn't seen before, one that she couldn't quite place. "Now we debrief, and figure out if this was a planned distraction, or simply a case of your ex figuring he'd be faster than we were."

"I'm very glad he wasn't," Mariah said. "Thank you for getting here so quickly."

"He shouldn't have gotten you out in the first place." Scowling, Gray glanced over at one of the SUVs, where the cop from Internal Affairs was standing guard over the turncoat officer, preventing anyone from talking to him. "Looks like the problems in the Bear Claw PD go deeper than we suspected."

"They took his family," Mariah said, her heart aching. "And in the end, he did the right thing."

"I would've found you even if he hadn't flagged me down," Gray said, transferring his attention to her, and she got the sense that he was saying more than that, whether he knew it or not.

In her heart, his words resonated as *I would've done whatever it took to find you.* And if that were simply her delusion—her needy, greedy wish to feel as though someone in this insane mess cared for her as a person rather than as a witness or an asset—then she acknowledged the weakness and kept it to herself.

Crossing her arms over her chest, she hugged herself. "You should look for his family."

"We already found them." His flat tone confirmed what the poor cop had guessed. Al-Jihad hadn't left them alive as potential witnesses. When the news brought another shiver, Gray scowled and shucked out of his ripped suit jacket. He tossed it to her. "Here. You're freezing."

She didn't argue. Nor did she take his gesture as a sign of anything but expediency. "Thanks." She pulled on the jacket, which was way too big for her but felt like heaven. Resisting the urge to snuggle, she took a deep breath and steadied herself to do something she knew she should've done before. "I need to go back up to the cabin."

That got his attention. "Why?"

"Because it's my home."

He shook his head. "You're smarter than that. They got in once, they can do it again."

She wrapped the suit coat tighter around her torso. "Not if you're there to protect me."

"I'm not a babysitter, and I'm not wasting my time playing bodyguard when I could be doing something more productive." He paused, eyes narrowing. "And you know that. Which means you think returning to the cabin will be productive."

She liked that he gave her credit, hated that he saw through her so easily. The transparency made her feel vulnerable, exposed. But she dipped her chin in a faint nod. "Earlier today, before you came into my room and…you know." She waved away what had happened between them, determined to play it as no big deal, although the depth of her response had been a very big deal to her. She continued, "Anyway, earlier, I was just dozing, drifting, and I heard Lee's voice whisper something about me helping them. And I'm pretty sure I remember him asking me about something, hounding me to tell him where something was. I'm not sure what."

Gray went still. "I thought you couldn't remember anything."

"I think it's coming back. I remember being tied up in the cabin, with him leaning over me."

"You were drugged. Your mind could be playing tricks on you."

"I'm convinced it was a real memory."

His eyes narrowed. "One that didn't surface during your debriefing? That's convenient."

Frustration sparked. The six hours she'd been questioned in a secure room deep within the Bear Claw PD prior to her transfer to the hospital had been difficult. With her lawyer present, she'd told the Feds everything she could remember about her captivity. She'd submitted to their blood tests, worked with a sketch artist to capture Brisbane's—or rather Felix Smith's—face, and even allowed Thorne Radcliffe, an FBI profiler with more than a touch of otherworldliness to his technique, to try hypnotizing her. "It's not my fault Thorne couldn't put me under. I told him before he started that I don't hypnotize well."

Actually, the mentalist had dubbed her "blocked" and "closed off," but Gray didn't call her on it. Instead, he shoved his hands into his pockets and rocked back on his heels, giving her the impression that she was finally getting through to him. "You didn't go under during hypnosis, yet you think visiting your cabin is going to shake the memories loose?"

"Not visiting. Staying there." She lifted her chin. "What happened today changes nothing. Unless al-Jihad has another source for whatever he wants from me. I still need protection. The cabin is a fortress. Lee only got to me last time because I shut down the perimeter in order to get back inside. You've got access to more men and better equipment."

"That's not a guarantee," he muttered.

"There aren't any guarantees here," she agreed. "You may not be able to keep me safe. I may not be able to figure out what Lee wants from me. But I think it's worth a try." Seeing that Gray was giving the idea serious consideration, she pressed, "What have you got to lose?"

That earned her a sharp look, but then his expression blanked. After a moment, he nodded. "Fine. We'll do it your way. I'll get Fax to help me clear it with Johnson, and collect the manpower and equipment we'll need to secure the cabin beyond your Mickey Mouse system."

Within twenty minutes, Gray got his superior's okay and preparations were underway.

Later that evening, almost seventy-two hours to the minute after Gray had driven Mariah down off the ridgeline, he drove her back up again.

The air in the truck was tense, and there was little conversation as the vehicle bumped up the access trail, followed by a chase car containing additional FBI agents and supplies. The knowledge that she and Gray weren't going to be alone up at the cabin should've been a relief to Mariah. Instead, she found herself wishing the other agents were gone, wishing Gray were gone, wishing she were alone and everything was back to normal. Which was impossible.

As the night-darkened woods passed on either side of the truck, she tried vainly to remember what Lee had said. What did the bombers want from her? They'd already taken so much from her. Why wasn't that enough?

*Think,* she told herself. *Focus!* But the memory eluded her, staying stubbornly out of reach.

She told herself that her failure to remember was the source of the leaden lump at the pit of her stomach. But as Gray turned his truck into the parking area beside her cabin and pulled up beside her Jeep, she couldn't help thinking that the sick feeling was more than her inability to recall what Lee had said.

"You ready?" Gray said, killing the engine and pocketing his keys.

She was tempted to tell him no, that she wasn't ready, that they should return to the city and try something else—questioning, more hypnosis, whatever it took. But they'd already tried those things and they hadn't worked. So rather than calling off the plan, as her instincts were clamoring for her to do, she nodded. "Ready."

At his signal she dropped down from the truck, then paused when the front door swung open and Fairfax stepped out onto the porch. The dark-haired agent looked past her and nodded to Gray. "All clear."

Gray urged her forward. "Let's get you inside."

She wanted to balk. Instead, she forced herself up the stairs and through the door into her cabin, her certainty growing with every step.

This had been a very bad idea.

# Chapter Seven

The moment he stepped through the front door he'd seen Lee step through only four days earlier, Gray found that Mariah's cabin might have been "all clear," but it still bore evidence of the recent siege.

The main room was a wide sweep running the length of the front of the cabin, with a sitting area to the right and a small kitchen to the left, separated by an island that doubled as both counter space and a dining table. The wall opposite the front door was broken up by two doors and a short hallway. From Mariah's description of her escape, he knew her bedroom was to the right, her spare room and bath to the left. The walls were polyurethaned logs intended to look far more rustic than they actually were, and the faux log-cabin theme was carried through in exposed beams and wide pine on the floor. The décor, such as it was, leaned toward the practical and comfortable. The main room had club-footed chairs and a cushionless sofa, upholstered in forest green, along with two rustic end tables, and several plain, functional lamps that lit the front rooms with stark yellow light. In the kitchen, the shelves stood empty. The floor was bare, the windows uncurtained, though the advance team had covered them with plain, functional blinds that would shield the cabin's occupants from view. On the counter rested several grocery bags, also courtesy of the advance team.

There were no personal touches, no hints of femininity, but Gray knew from the reports—and his own instincts—that those touches had been there before Lee's arrival. More, he knew in his gut that Mariah would've made her space a home, a nest.

He'd seen the way she'd maintained order even in her hospital room. She had kept the items on her bedside table and in the bathroom each in the place she'd assigned them. She was neat and organized, not in the way of someone who was obsessed with it, but more like someone who'd had so many upheavals in her life that she'd learned to control what pieces of it she could.

He imagined that she'd taken care with her small living space. He could only assume that seeing her home stripped bare, as it was now, would hurt her.

He was tempted to block her from entering, to take her back down to the city and watch over her there— or, even better, lock her into a safe house until Mawadi and the others had been dealt with.

But that was the irrational part of him talking, the part that had gotten so caught up in guilting himself over their kiss that he hadn't been at his post when the turncoat cop had abducted her from the hospital. And although that situation had worked out, thanks to a GPS and some major strokes of luck, it only confirmed what his rational, trained side had been telling him since that first moment he'd kissed her and nearly lost himself. Or hell, since the moment he'd plastered himself atop her out in the woods beyond the cabin, shielding her from discovery, and had been all but derailed by the feel of her body beneath his.

She was trouble, and the two of them together were a bad mix.

There was chemistry, yes—a whole lot of chemistry, though she was nothing like the soft, feminine women he was typically drawn to. And he was even tempted to like her from time to time, when he didn't want to strangle her for being stubborn and insisting on challenging him at every turn. But none of that was pertinent to the case at hand, was it? He had to think like a special agent on this one. She was an asset, nothing more. The next time he forgot that and let her distract him, she could very well end up dead. And if she died without remembering what Lee wanted from her, then the next terror attack, and the hundreds—maybe even thousands—of lives lost, would be on his head.

So instead of sparing her the sight of what her ex had done to her home, he stepped aside and beckoned her inside. "Come on. Let's do this."

She moved through the front door and stopped short. Her eyes went blank for a second, then flooded with emotion. "Oh. It's so…empty." She looked around, her breath catching. "Where are all my pictures? The rugs are gone, the pillows, everything." She turned to him. "Did the CSIs really need to take everything?"

"They didn't." His voice came out flat as he forced himself to keep the necessary distance. "I had a cleaning crew come in and clear out everything that Lee and Brisbane wrecked while they were staying here. The damaged stuff is bagged and tagged outside." According to the reports, that accounted for just about everything in the cabin except the furniture. "You can go through it later, but the cleaners said almost all of it was beyond salvage."

The men—or, most likely, in Gray's opinion, Lee—had used the sofa cushions for target practice, smashed the photographs, urinated on the rugs, torn through her clothing and photographic equipment, and wrecked almost everything else that could be wrecked. The couch and chairs had taken some hits, too, but the cleaners had been able to remove the worst of the stains. It would be up to Mariah whether she wanted to keep those pieces.

Not that she needed to know those details right now. The violation she was feeling showed in her eyes, and in the stiff tension in her body. She was wearing jeans and a pale amber sweater that earlier in the day had picked up the color in her eyes and the highlights in her dark, curly hair. Now, though, the color only served to emphasize the deathly pallor of her face, giving her an air of fragile vulnerability, and he was used to her being neither fragile nor vulnerable.

For a second she looked small and delicate, which kicked at every protective urge Gray had ever possessed, threatening to override his better judgment. He'd actually taken two steps toward her before she turned and pinned him with a look.

"No." The word was soft, but underlaid with steel. Tears glistened in her eyes, but her voice held only determination when she said, "You don't get to have it both ways. You don't get to touch me when you feel like it, then turn around and tell me it's all about the case. You don't want to be attracted to me, don't want to be with me. I get that. Well, guess what? Given a choice in the matter, I wouldn't pick you, either. Which should make this much easier than it would've been otherwise." She looked past him to the open door. "Are the others coming in?"

He reached back without looking and swung the door shut. "Nope. They'll form a perimeter outside." It wasn't SOP, but it was what Gray had insisted on. Not because he wanted to spend time alone with her in the small cabin, but because he'd thought it would be easier for her that way, without five other agents lurking in the cabin.

She looked at him for a long moment, then surprised him by nodding. "Thanks. Good call. The more space I've got to myself, the more likely I'll be able to remember what Lee said."

That was pretty much what Gray had been thinking, which made him wish he didn't understand her as well as he was coming to. In his business, detachment was key.

Needing some crucial distance, he pulled out his cell and checked the time. "It's nearly midnight. We should move some furniture, get some sleep." He prowled across the main room to check out the two back bedrooms. They were both equally small, but one was crammed full of furniture, while the other held only a bare mattress on a bed frame that was pushed up against the wall, right below a shiny new eyebolt that'd been screwed deep into one of the polyurethaned logs.

Gray went rigid with raw fury as he pictured Mariah lying there, bound, terrified and chained to the wall, terrorized by the man she'd thought she loved.

This time, he gave in to the urge to block the doorway. He turned and found Mariah close behind him. Scowling, he said, "You'll sleep in the main room or the other bedroom."

He halfway expected an argument, halfway expected relief. He hadn't expected her eyes to soften just a hint, or her lips to turn up at the corners in a sad smile.

"I appreciate the thought. Seriously. But we both know the best way for me to remember is to put myself in the same situation I was in when I heard Lee the first time." She nudged him aside, and Gray gave way because she was right, dammit.

She moved to the center of the room, then stopped and stood, staring at the bed. The overhead bulb illuminated the scene in stark yellow light that did nothing to blunt the impact of a bedroom that had been turned into a cell.

When she turned and looked at him, Gray saw the memories in her eyes, and the despair. "Mariah," he began, but then stopped, because what could he say? She was right about a number of things, not the least of them that she needed to stay in that bed, and he needed to keep his hands off her if he didn't intend to follow through on what was—or could be—between them.

She nodded as if he'd said those things aloud. "Yeah. I know." Squaring her shoulders, she said, "Did he leave me any sheets and pillows?"

"I had an agent pick up supplies, bedding included. The advance team left the bags in the spare room."

"In other words, no, he didn't leave me anything except the walls and some furniture." She nodded as if she'd expected the answer, though her expression was bleak and her voice very soft and sad when she said, "Lee has a mean streak. Heck, that's practically all he is—one big mean streak. I didn't see it until after we were married. That's going to haunt me, I expect, until the day I die. If I had seen it, if I had done something—"

"Don't," Gray interrupted. He moved in closer to her, not to soothe, but so she would know that he meant every word. "First off, there was no way you could've known; he was playing a role, and he's smart and ruthless enough to pull it off." Gray knew that for a fact, having watched the bastard nearly charm a jury into acquitting him. "Second, if your gut had warned you off him in the beginning, he would've just moved on to someone else, used someone else. That would've changed your life, yes, but it wouldn't have stopped the bombing. Al-Jihad doesn't open himself to risk by having just one plan—he has backups upon backups. You were one piece of a larger whole. And third, if you'd figured it out and turned Lee in, there's no telling what would have happened. Maybe the authorities would've traced him back to al-Jihad before the bombing. Probably not, though. And you know what one thing you can be sure of? If you'd turned him in, you wouldn't be here right now."

He hadn't meant to put it so bluntly, but there it was. She'd survived her marriage only because she'd withdrawn into herself and presented such a minimal threat to Mawadi's plans that it hadn't been necessary to kill her beforehand. And then she'd gotten very, very lucky. On the day of the bombing, Lee had arranged to meet her at one of the Santa's thrones. She'd been delayed by traffic just long enough so that she arrived at the mall late. She'd been in the parking lot when the bombs went off.

"You're right." She nodded, pale but determined. "And I'm going to make him sorry he ever pulled me into this. I'd like to say he's going to be sorry for what he's done, but I don't think he's capable of that." Features set, she headed out of the room. "I'm going to make the bed, at least. I may have to sleep in here, but I don't have to do it on a bare mattress." She turned back in the doorway. "You want the foldout in the spare room or the couch in the living room? If you want the foldout, we'll have to shift some furniture around in the office. They certainly jammed stuff in there." Her tone was matter-of-fact, but he could see the effort it took her to maintain that practical, no-nonsense front. He sensed that she needed to crumble, but she'd be damned if she'd do it in front of him.

He wanted to soothe, but he didn't have the right. So he dipped his chin, acknowledging all of it, and said, "I'll bunk down on the couch."

Not that he'd be sleeping much. He could go days without sleep on assignment and intended to do exactly that on this job. It wasn't that he distrusted the perimeter the other agents had set up, per se. It was more that he'd stayed alive up to that point by virtue of not trusting anyone but himself. According to Stacy, that was one of the things that had torpedoed their marriage, which by extension meant it had begun the domino effect that had put him and the others in Colorado for the bombings. But so what? His lack of trust might have indirectly put him in the current situation, but it was going to damn well get him out of it intact, and he was bringing Mariah out safely with him.

Although she'd seemed to read his thoughts from his expressions a few times before, this time she took his words at face value, simply nodding and turning away. "I'll go see what your agents left us."

Gray didn't follow her out. He crossed the room, shoved her bed out of the way and went to work on the eyebolt. Cursing Mawadi to hell and back, he used the spare clip from his 9 mm as leverage to unscrew the hardware from its bite in the heavy log wall. The bolt resisted at first; it'd been driven deep with what he imagined had been Mawadi's desire for revenge against the woman who'd dared to divorce him.

But Gray was fueled by an equal measure of anger, and hatred for men like Mawadi, who killed because it entertained them, or like al-Jihad, who killed because their own warped, twisted sense of right and wrong demanded it. And, as the bolt finally came free of the wood and clattered to the floor beneath the bed, Gray knew he was currently being compelled by another, equally hot emotion.

He needed to know that Mariah wouldn't be staring at that damn eyebolt as she tried to remember what her ex had said to her.

Stirred up, ticked off and feeling as though he were about to explode, Gray swept up the bolt from under the bed and stalked through the crowded spare room to the back exit, through which Mariah had escaped four days ago—four days that seemed like so much longer. He was aware of her watching him, wide-eyed, as he yanked open the door, waved for the perimeter guards to stand down, and hurled the eyebolt outside.

Then he slammed and locked the door, and headed back out into the main room. Edgy, greedy need licked along his nerve endings like fire, and he knew if he didn't get some space, he wasn't going to like what happened next. But where the hell was he supposed to get space when he was locked in with just the person he needed to get away from?

"Gray," she said from behind him.

He held up a hand to forestall whatever was coming next, but didn't look back at her because he wasn't sure what would happen if she kept talking. "Not now. Please, Mariah, not now. Just go to sleep. We'll talk in the morning."

He expected an argument, and a hard, hot piece of him might have welcomed it. But for the first time since he'd met her, she took the coward's way out, saying only, "Good night, then."

He held himself still, standing rigid in the center of the main room until he heard her bedroom door close.

Then he dropped down onto the sofa, put his head in his hands, and tried to remember his damn priorities. He wasn't there for her. She was there to help him bring down Mawadi and the others, nothing more. There couldn't be anything more, he reminded himself. Not until he'd taken care of the business at hand. And then? Well, then he and Mariah would go their separate ways.

He knew from personal experience that physical attraction didn't make a solid foundation for a lasting relationship when the two people involved had nothing but chemistry in common.

MARIAH SLEPT FITFULLY, her slumber broken up by dream fragments and nightmares. Each time she awakened, she tried to relax, tried to lull herself into a state where she could call forth Lee's questions, but to no avail. Maybe she was trying too hard. Who knew? All she knew for sure was that she was wide awake before dawn, physically exhausted but mentally restless.

The knowledge that Gray was out in the main room kept her in bed for longer than she would've stayed there otherwise, partly because she didn't want to wake him if he were sleeping, and partly because she didn't want to deal with him, period. He made her feel so many contradictory things all at once, in one big messy knot of uncertainty. She felt safe with him, yet vulnerable; empowered yet weak; sometimes needy and feminine, other times practical and unsexy. She didn't know who she was around him, didn't know how to act.

She lay in her bare bedroom, replaying the kiss they had shared, remembering the sensations he'd sparked, and the emotions.

She had come into her marriage relatively inexperienced, and while sex with Lee had been pleasant at first, even exciting at times, those good times had quickly shifted to power plays and manipulation. It had taken her months to figure out what had changed, and longer than that after the bombings and her quickie divorce to separate out the guilt from the sex and rationally work through what he'd done to her, and how. She'd consulted a therapist, and though it had profoundly unsettled her to share intimate details with a stranger, the sessions had helped her find her center and her balance.

She didn't fear sex, she'd decided, but neither had she desired it for some time. The therapist had assured her that her libido would return eventually. It was just her luck the damn thing had decided to come back online now, and with a totally unsuitable man. Still, she couldn't escape the memory of how his mouth had felt against hers, how his lips had felt on her skin. As they'd kissed, he'd been focused only on her, and on the heat they'd made together.

And she so wasn't getting any closer to remembering what Lee wanted from her, lying there thinking of another, far better—though no less complicated—man.

Muttering under her breath, she got up, got dressed in yesterday's clothes, used the bathroom and then headed for the kitchen, in need of a serious caffeine hit to counteract the effects of the long night and the preceding days.

A light was on in the main room, though Gray appeared to be asleep, lying on his back in a sprawl of leashed male strength. He'd swapped his ruined suit for worn jeans and a long-sleeved shirt that gapped open at the throat, and he wore thick socks against the snap in the mountain air. His boots sat close at hand and his holstered weapon rested on an end table. The sight was more reassuring than intimidating, though Mariah found it a bit of both.

"Bad dreams?" he said, sounding wide awake, though he didn't open his eyes or otherwise move.

She was grateful he'd kept his eyes closed; she didn't want to start the day by being caught staring. Then again, the fact that she'd stopped dead in the middle of the living room had probably been a good clue.

"I wouldn't mind the bad dreams if they were at all productive," she answered. Forcing herself to get moving rather than watching him any longer, she tossed over her shoulder, "You want coffee?"

His jaw went tight, and something that looked like anger flashed in his eyes when they opened. "I'll fend for myself." He rose and headed for the bathroom, seeming to have come fully awake in an instant. When he returned to the main room, he pulled on his boots, donned his holster and grabbed the jacket he'd hung near the front door. "I'm going to check in with the others. Be back in a few."

"Will it bother you if I make enough breakfast for everyone?" she asked, having gotten a definite edge off his tone when he'd turned down her offer of coffee.

"Suit yourself." He didn't look at her as he unlocked the front door, snapped a quick radio check at the team outside and left, closing the door behind him with an emphatic thunk of wood on wood.

When he was gone, the air should've felt softer and less tense to Mariah. She should've welcomed the few minutes of privacy, the moment to be alone. Instead, the cabin felt empty, and the atmosphere hummed with the same tension as before, only worse now, as though her psyche were determined to make her acknowledge that things had changed, that maybe being alone wasn't what she wanted anymore.

But she'd fallen into that trap once before, following the urges to New York, and from there into marriage. She'd learned her lesson, hadn't she?

Working on autopilot, she made coffee, grimacing when she pawed through the grocery bags and checked the refrigerator. The brands weren't the ones she would have chosen, the selection somewhat haphazard, serving to drive home the reality she'd been trying to avoid facing since the previous night, when she'd stepped inside the cabin and felt like the space wasn't hers anymore. Lee had destroyed her photos and knick-knacks. He'd eaten her food, sat on her furniture and done heaven only knew what else to her personal space. And whatever the crime-scene analysts hadn't needed, the cleaners had taken care of. Her home had been stripped of character, her touch erased, leaving her to start over yet again.

But when tears threatened to blur her vision, she dashed them away, irritated with herself. "They're just things. Get over it."

Except Lee hadn't taken only her things. He'd also taken a big chunk of her self-respect and her ability to trust, and he'd driven a deeper wedge between her and her parents. They hadn't left because they'd needed to get away from Bear Claw. They'd left because they'd wanted to get away from her and the intrusive media presence she'd brought into their lives. She'd tried not to blame them, but just as they'd stayed on the road when she'd wanted to settle down, and settled down just as she was ready to leave the nest, her parents had done what they needed for each other, not what she'd needed from them.

That wasn't news, or even much of a surprise, but it had stung nonetheless. Was it so much to ask that someone care for her for her own sake?

"And aren't we feeling self-pitying this morning?" she said aloud. "Get over it. You're alive and in protective custody, and sooner or later this thing is going to break." God willing. And when it did, when Lee and al-Jihad and the rest of them were all off the street, then she'd be free to start over. Again.

Needing to keep busy while her brain churned, she pulled together a basic breakfast from the supplies at hand, and refilled the coffeemaker after she'd downed her second cup. By the time Gray returned, she had prepared scrambled eggs and toasted bagels, and found paper plates and plastic utensils among the bagged supplies. She was trying not to think about what Lee had probably done to her dishes. They had been inexpensive warehouse-store purchases, but she'd liked the repeating motifs of birds and pinecones.

Gesturing with the package of plates, she said, "Can I impose on you to take these outside, or can the agents take turns coming in or something?

Gray scowled, temper lighting his eyes. "I told you we'd fend for ourselves."

She would've snapped in response, except that she

thought she caught a thread of something else beneath the anger, a hint that looked almost like desperation, and told her this wasn't about eggs, or even the case. Setting down the plates, she crossed to the coffeepot, very deliberately poured a second mug and carried it over to him. She held it out, partly a peace offering, partly a dare. "No," she said, keeping her tone reasonable, "you said I should suit myself, which I did, by making breakfast for everyone."

He stared down at her for a long moment. Then he muttered something under his breath, and took the coffee. "Seriously, it's not your responsibility to feed us."

"I need to do something, or I'll go insane," she said reasonably. At least she thought it was reasonable.

He dipped his head in a half nod. "That much I get. Okay. Thanks. I'll let them know they can come in on a rotation." But he didn't leave, didn't turn away, just stood there holding the mug of coffee, staring down at her.

Mariah held her ground, refusing the sudden urge to fuss with her hair or check if she had a smattering of bagel crumbs on her cheek. The damn electricity that had gotten them in trouble before sparked in the air between them now, as his expression went from fierce and annoyed to something softer. The sight of it brought a warm twist low in her belly, and her voice threatened to shake when she said, "If you're trying to come up with an apology for being an ass, don't worry about it. This isn't exactly a normal situation."

"Not an apology," he said, "an explanation for why I'm not comfortable with the whole breakfast thing."

"You've got a lifelong bacheloresque fear of having a woman cook you breakfast?" she asked, and for the first time she realized that while he knew some of the most intimate details of her life, she knew almost nothing about his.

"I was married," he said, surprising her because she'd pegged him as the "never been married, never wanted to be married" type. He continued, "More than that, I liked being married. I liked coming down and smelling coffee and toast, or getting up first and putting something together for the two of us. That's something I miss." He paused. "The last time anyone made me breakfast was the morning of the bombings."

Mariah sucked in a breath as the world closed in around her. "Your wife was in one of the malls?"

He shook his head, but his expression didn't clear. "No, Stacy's alive and well, remarried and living in L.A. We'd just gotten separated—it was her idea, though I think we both knew it wasn't working. I went to stay with friends out here in Colorado—my college roommate, Ken, his wife, Trish, and their six-month-old baby, Catherine. My goddaughter." He paused. Mariah would've said something, but all of the air seemed to have been sucked from her lungs, rendering her silent as he continued, "They wanted to cheer me up, so Trish made a big breakfast late that morning, we went and picked out a Christmas tree and then we headed over to the local mall so they could take Catherine's picture with Santa." He broke off then and took a long swallow of the scalding-hot coffee, but didn't seem to notice the heat.

"Gray," Mariah began.

"I was standing in line with them," he continued as if she hadn't spoken, "and God help me, I was frustrated as hell, and getting mean. I was jealous of Ken—the guy who'd been my wingman in college, my good friend in the years since. He was so damn happy, he and Trish were so good together, and baby Catherine was so perfect…I couldn't take it anymore. I said something to them—I don't even remember what—and I took off. I just needed a minute alone, needed to find a way to stop hating my buddy for having everything that I wanted." He spread his hands away from his body and looked at her, hollow-eyed. "I was sitting on a bench near this fountain, maybe a few hundred yards away, when the bomb went off."

Mariah would've touched him, would've soothed him if she could've figured out how. But he looked so closed off, standing there with pain in his eyes and his body language telling her to keep away, that he didn't want sympathy or understanding, didn't want anything but to punish himself.

"Gray," she said again.

This time he heard her. He looked at her, seeming to see her now, and his voice went harsh when he said, "So yeah, that's an apology for my being less than gracious over your offer of breakfast. And it's an explanation for a whole bunch of other things, isn't it?"

"You're not going to move on until you're sure your friends have gotten justice," she said, making it a statement rather than a question. Her chest ached for a family she hadn't known, and Gray who'd suffered one blow on top of another, for no other reason than he'd been in the wrong place at the wrong time.

In that, she thought, they finally had something in common. Neither of them had done the wrong thing to begin with, but the domino effect of decisions they'd made had led to terrible consequences nonetheless.

"The baby was partly shielded by her parents' bodies," he said, his voice raw. "I got her out and pulled rank to get her on the first ambulance out of there, triage be damned. They tried…I know they tried. I was sitting outside the PICU when she passed twenty-two hours later. I've been trying to wipe al-Jihad and his network off the face of the planet ever since, and I don't intend to stop until I do it, or die trying."

He said the latter so matter-of-factly that she believed, with absolute certainty, that he would willingly lose his own life if he could be sure of taking the terrorists with him.

What would it be like, she wondered, to be the focus of an emotion that intense, coming from a man capable of such feeling?

"I'm sorry," he said, "that was probably way more than you wanted or needed to know." He turned away, heading for the door. "I'll tell the others to come in and get food. Stay put for an hour and don't give them any grief, okay? I need to walk."

She told herself to let him go, that it would be better for both of them if she did. Instead, she said, "Wait."

He paused, glancing back. "Yeah?"

"I'm coming with you. You don't know these woods they way I do."

His eyes went unreadable. "Thanks for the concern, but I found my way up here just fine the other day. Trust me, I won't get lost."

"No, but you won't find what you're looking for, either."

"Which is what?"

"Peace," she said simply. "A place where you can sit and think, or clear your mind and just let yourself forget for a little while." She almost held out a hand to him, but thought better of it and walked past him to grab a jacket and shove her feet into a pair of hiking boots.

"You're not leaving the cabin," he said, but it was a weak protest.

"Bring the others if you want, or bring some of them and leave the rest here to guard our backs," she said, suddenly realizing that she needed to make the visit for her own purposes as well. "I really think we should go. I think…I'm sure that if I can just clear my head, I'll be able to remember what Lee said. I can't do that here after all. Maybe I'll be able to do it where we're going."

"Where is that?" he asked, and she knew she had him.

Now she did hold out a hand to him. "Come on. I'll show you."

## Chapter Eight

Protocol said they should stay in the cabin, but as far as Gray was concerned, protocol—or rather Johnson's stubborn adherence to protocol regardless of the situation—had hampered the investigation too much for too long.

Besides, Johnson was off chasing other leads. The SAC hadn't said as much, but Gray knew his boss held little hope of Mariah being able to help at this point. That was why Johnson had agreed so readily to the op up at the ridgeline cabin, and why he'd assigned a handful of relatively junior agents to the protective detail. Which was just fine as far as Gray was concerned, because it gave him greater leeway than he would've had otherwise—including the leverage to fall in with Mariah's plan of hiking out into the woods to meditate. If they were lucky, it'd smooth out the edges they were both feeling, allowing her to relax and access her memories of being incarcerated.

He was rationalizing—he knew it. Logic dictated that they should stay put in the cabin, that Mariah should try working with the self-hypnosis protocols the profiler, Thorne, had given her. Instead, they were going for a damn walk, not just because Mariah thought it would help her remember, but because he'd dumped his story on her, and in the aftermath she'd recognized that if he didn't get out of the cabin, didn't burn off some of the restless, edgy energy that always gathered when he thought about the day of the bombing, the consequences could be dire.

He'd thought he had the memories and the rage under control. Apparently, he'd been dead wrong.

Mariah led the way along the narrow, wooded trail, which was on a slight upgrade that headed up the mountain. Gray hiked immediately behind and off to the right of her, keeping a sharp eye on the scene ahead of them, ready to shield her if necessary. Behind him ranged three of the junior agents, one of whom had clearly let his gym time lag. Gray could hear the guy puffing with the effort of the climb, and felt zero sympathy.

They were all on high alert, though there had been no sign of anyone else in the woods. They'd barely seen any wildlife, either, just trees and more trees, with glimpses of the leaden gray sky becoming more frequent as they climbed higher and the forest thinned slightly.

Gray's blood hummed with tension and exertion, clearing his mind and sharpening his senses.

The dull snap of the damp leaves and twigs beneath their boots was a rhythmic counterpoint to the rasp of their breaths, occasionally highlighted by the cry of a gliding hawk or eagle. The air moved through the treetops in a steady flow, forming a whisper of background noise that took the edges off the churned-up feelings inside him. The air smelled of pine and rain, with an overtone of rot from the fallen trees that littered the forest floor, slowly returning to the soil they'd sprung from. And though Gray knew it was his imagination, or wishful thinking that everything could've been different between them, as he walked, he swore he could taste Mariah on his lips. They'd only kissed once, but her feel and flavor were locked into his sensory memory.

Ahead of him, she walked with loose, swinging strides. She didn't look around, keeping her attention fixed on the root-strewn trail, but somehow he knew she was completely aware of her surroundings, fully tuned in to the forest.

After a half hour or so, she turned off the path and picked her way up a steep incline, using gnarled pine roots as footholds. When Gray followed, he saw that the roots she'd used were worn smooth. And when she paused on a narrow ledge and waited for him to catch up, he found that she'd led him to a small cave that had been invisible from below, shielded by overgrown scrub and a trick of light and angles.

"The others should wait here," she said. "It's tight quarters in the cave. It'll be too crowded and distracting with five of us in there."

Gray couldn't argue, especially after the three junior agents had reached the ledge, forcing him to crowd her practically into the cave mouth. But he frowned. "There's no way your ex could know about this place?"

She shook her head. "I moved here after he was

locked up, and this cave isn't on any of the maps that I'm aware of. It's not part of any of the old mine systems, and we're way off the beaten tourist path."

"You found it," he pointed out.

She glanced at him and hesitated a moment, as if weighing her answer. Then she said, "I told you how my parents were always moving around? Well, my grandfather didn't—he lived in Montana, in a set of woods not unlike these. I spent as much time there as my folks would let me, and whenever I visited, Grandpa took me out hiking. In part, I think he was trying to wear me out so I'd stop talking—I loved to talk to him, because it felt like he really listened." She paused and flicked a glance beyond Gray to the other agents. Lifting a shoulder in a self-conscious half shrug, she finished, "Anyway, he was a woodsman from way back, sometimes hunting wildlife, though mostly shooting with his camera by the time I came along. He taught me how to read the woods, and how to find my way home."

Gray wanted to tell her to clue him in on that last part, because it had been a long time since he'd been someplace that felt like home. That had been a large part of his snappishness that morning—the realization that coming into her cabin and finding her in the kitchen, surrounded by the smells of morning and warmth, had felt far too natural, bringing a wistful ache.

They were different in more ways than he could count. So why did it sometimes seem as if they clicked on levels he hadn't even known would get to him?

"It's not safe," one of the junior agents said from

behind him. It took Gray a moment to figure out that the other man was talking about the cave.

"We'll be fine," Gray said, before he realized that he'd made the decision. He glanced back at the others. "Stay here and keep watch. I doubt the radios will work in the cave, so if we get in trouble, we'll fire a couple of warning shots. If we're not back in three hours, come in after us." He fixed the third, lagging agent with a look. "And while you're waiting, maybe you can talk to these guys about joining a damn gym." When he turned back to Mariah, he caught the hint of a grin. "What?"

"For a second there, you sounded like your boss."

Gray shuddered. "Please." Gesturing to the cave, he said, "Lead on."

She pulled a midsized flashlight out of her back pocket. Snapping it on, she directed the yellow cone of light into the cave. "Follow me."

With a final warning look at the junior agents, whom he suspected had also been tasked with keeping tabs on him for Johnson's benefit, Gray ducked through the scrub guarding the cave mouth and moved inside.

The temperature immediately dropped a good ten degrees and the air dampened, sending a shiver down the back of his neck. The cave walls were raw and uneven, arching up and over him by a foot or so. The floor was a craggy mix of stone and dirt, the latter of which had been flattened in places by a woman's footprints, suggesting that Mariah came here often.

In a dozen long strides, he caught up with her as she forged ahead down the narrow arcade formed by the cave. "No offense, but this isn't exactly my idea of a meditation spot." He pitched his voice low, but the sound bounced off the rock walls, making it seem as though he'd shouted.

"Patience, Grasshopper. And silence is a virtue."

It surprised him to realize that he, a man who most often kept his own counsel, wanted to talk, the words coming from the fine hum of energy that ran through him. He didn't think it was nerves, exactly, but he didn't know what else to call it. Awareness, maybe, or the gut-deep sense that something important was about to happen.

He'd felt the same way once or twice on assignment, when his instincts had warned him that things were going south. He hadn't had any premonition the day of the bombing, though, or the day he'd ignored another agent's message and had nearly gotten a stadium full of innocents killed. Was it any wonder he didn't trust his own instincts? They sure as hell hadn't proven themselves when it counted.

"Through here," Mariah said, poking her head into what looked like a crack in the wall of the main cave. "Watch your head."

A hint of claustrophobia kicked in. "I don't know—"

"It opens up a short way in," she called back, her voice echoing strangely from within the small niche.

"I don't like feeling trapped."

"Who does? It's worth it, I promise. Trust me."

He wondered if she understood how rarely he trusted anything but rock-solid evidence. He didn't even trust himself half the time. Yet still, he ducked and followed, crab-walking toward the faint yellow glow of her flashlight, hoping to hell she'd considered the fact that he was considerably larger than she was.

The tight fit brought a second, stronger surge of claustrophobia, but he kept going, ignoring the way the rock touched him on all sides and snagged at his clothing. Moments later, he realized that he wasn't following the flashlight at all. He was headed toward daylight. Beyond, he could hear the sound of running water and the trill of a songbird.

The cave opening became clear, partly blocked by Mariah's body, which was silhouetted against the light. When he reached her, she took his hand, the gesture somehow managing not to bump up against the boundaries they'd set, seeming friendly rather than sexual, as if saying they were in this together. "Come on," she urged. "Take a look."

She drew him through the opening, onto another stone ledge like the one they'd come from. Only this one didn't overlook a forest path, he saw when he straightened to his full height. It overlooked a mountain paradise.

The small bowl of grass-covered earth was bounded on all sides by high rock walls, though dark niches here and there suggested that their particular cave wasn't the only way in or out. In almost the exact center of the bowl, a pool of water formed a nearly perfect circle, fed by a tall, cascading waterfall that accounted for the roaring noise. At the opposite side, a narrow outflow disappeared between a pair of rock slabs that leaned into each other, forming a small triangular gap at their bases.

The ledge where Mariah and Gray stood was twenty, maybe thirty feet up from the grassy floor, giving them a breathtaking vantage point without distancing them from the splendor of the view.

"What do you think?" Mariah asked softly, not looking at him.

"You promised me peace," he replied, his voice not echoing now that they were back outside. "I'd say you delivered." He could practically feel the tension melt away from him, thought he felt the same from her through their joined hands.

"Come on." She tugged him along the ledge, to where a treacherous-looking path wound down to the grassy floor.

He followed without protest, not feeling trapped anymore, but feeling humbled and somehow insignificant. Human. Very unlike the person he'd become over the past few years, who was more special agent than man, and who walked the thin line between justice and vigilantism.

She led him to the edge of the pool, where a flat rock hung over like a wide diving platform. Instead of the cool of the cave, the air beside the water was mild, and the spray from the cataract felt warm on the exposed skin of his hands and face.

"Is there a hot spring underneath?" he asked, pitching his voice so Mariah could hear him over the thunder of water.

She lifted her free hand in a gesture of "Who knows?" "Either that or the bowl somehow creates a miniclimate of its own. I'm a photographer, not a scientist. The water's warm, that's for sure."

Which reminded him of something that got his gut twinging. "The pictures Lee wrecked. Were they of this place? Could he follow them here?"

She shook her head. "No, those were older pictures, ones I'd taken before I met Lee. Once he and I got married, there never seemed to be time for me to shoot pictures, or I was never in the mood. It wasn't until later that I realized that was another way he was controlling me. Then, after the attacks there was the trial and all the problems with my parents and the media, and there was no way I could see beauty in the world the way I used to." She paused. "I only started taking pictures again a few months ago, after I found this place. It gave me…perspective, I guess you could say. Maybe it'll do the same for you."

*And maybe it'll help you remember,* he thought about saying, but didn't because he recognized the urge for what it was: a cop-out, a pretense that this was about the case rather than the two of them, and the simpatico connection that had grown between them whether either of them liked it or not. So rather than deflecting the moment, he gave in to it, dropping down to sit at the edge of the warm stone overhang, where a natural depression formed a place where they could lean back comfortably. He tugged her down beside him, no words seeming necessary.

They sat there for a long moment, watching the waterfall. The liquid curtain was both hypnotic in its relentless rhythm and surprising in the endless variety of patterns that arose from water falling along the exact same path.

After a while, he said softly, "I don't remember the last time I talked about Ken, Trish and the baby. I guess

I got tired of everyone telling me their deaths were on al-Jihad and his people, not on me. But the whole mall trip was Trish's idea of how to get me out of my own head. She said she just wanted to see me smile."

"What would they say if they saw you now?"

Gray winced at the question he'd consciously avoided asking himself more than once before. "Doesn't matter. They're dead."

"You're not."

"Aren't you supposed to be meditating?"

She shot him a "gotcha" look from beneath her lashes, but fell silent and returned her attention to the waterfall.

Gray watched the patterns of the cataract, and the tumbling swirls of impact where the fall met the pond. The moist, warm air melted into him, relaxing him, and the skimming patterns, coupled with the thunderous white noise of the waterfall, made him dizzy, then slid him toward a light doze.

He didn't mean to fall asleep, didn't know how long he was out, but when he awakened the cloud cover had broken and sunlight was streaming down, lighting the glen and refracting through the mists that gathered where the waterfall hit the pool below. Rainbows grew from the mists, making him think he was still dreaming because in his experience, such beauty was the province of movies and fantasy, not the hard, bloody grit of the real world.

It wasn't just the mist or the scenery, either. It was the woman beside him.

Mariah lay on her side facing him, propped up on

one elbow, looking down at him expectantly, as though she'd been the one to wake him. Her dark hair was a riot of moisture-sprung curls, and her lips were wet and full, as they'd been the day before, right after he'd tangled with her in a kiss that they'd both agreed was a mistake, but that had felt like anything but.

When their eyes connected, the sun warmed a degree, and the rainbows gleamed a fraction brighter, which only confirmed what he'd suspected—that this was a dream. And because it was a dream, it was supremely natural for him to reach up to her, and for her to lean down, so they met halfway in a kiss that might not make sense in the real world, but was exactly right in this one.

MARIAH SAW THE FUZZY warmth in his eyes, and knew he hadn't fully awakened when he reached for her, when he kissed her.

On one level she knew she should stop him, that they had tried this, and it hadn't left either of them in a good place. But the waterfall always left her warm and soft, and sharing this spot with him had wound up feeling far more intimate than she'd expected or intended. She'd meant to offer him a bit of peace to counteract the grief she'd seen in his face when he'd spoken of his dead friends. She'd also meant to find some peace for herself, and maybe use it to dredge up darker memories.

She'd found the peace but not the memory, and maybe it was partly that frustration that had her leaning into him and allowing the kiss. Welcoming it. Returning it. But that was only part of what had her twining her arms around his neck and shifting so they almost touched, so the air between them heated with the promise of that touch.

The rest was simple desire. Which wasn't simple at all.

Need spun through her, spiraling higher when he shifted against her, so his chest dragged against the sensitized tips of her breasts and his strong thighs tangled with her legs. She moaned, the soft sound carrying over the crash of the waterfall and jolting her to new awareness of what they were doing, and where.

More important, she remembered what was waiting for them back out in reality—namely, the knowledge that they weren't a good fit, and the presence of larger stakes, not just for the two of them but for the innocents she'd failed before. And in remembering that, she remembered something else: a happy image of a smiling clown face.

Adrenaline slashed through her. Breaking the kiss, she pulled back, grinning. "I think I know what Lee wants."

As a mood killer, that statement ranked pretty high.

Gray went very still, though she felt the tension in his body and the rapid beat of his pulse. His eyes darkened with something akin to regret. "For a second, I thought this was a hell of a dream."

"Sorry."

"Me, too." He disengaged and rolled away from her to lie on his back for a moment, breathing deeply, his eyes closed in concentration. When he opened them again, she saw not the man, but the soldier. "What did he say to you?"

She shook her head. "I can't remember precisely what he said. But I was sitting here doing some of the breathing exercises that profiler showed me, just letting myself drift, and I started getting panicky, and heard myself saying, 'No, no, no!'"

She didn't realize that she'd balled her hands into fists until she felt him take one in his own and uncurl her fingers to tangle them with his in a gesture that was more supportive than sexual, but brought a warm, steadying glow nonetheless. "I'm here," Gray said simply. "He's not. You're safe."

And because she was safe in this insulated place, with this good-hearted though closed-off man, in this moment in time, she was able to continue. "Just now, I saw an image, and I suddenly knew what he'd been asking me about. It was this little statuette I used to have, a ceramic figurine of a clown I kept in my curio cabinet."

Gray frowned. "Why would he want a piece of china?"

She shook her head, baffled. "I don't know. Maybe because it was one of the few things I ever stood up to him on. He didn't like it, thought it was silly and juvenile. After we got married and moved into the new house—I know, how old-fashioned, that we didn't live together first?—he told me to get rid of it a few times. I argued with him, and he let me keep it. For the longest time, though, I thought that was where the problems started in our marriage, with that damn ceramic clown."

Gray squeezed her fingers, bringing her attention to

him. "What, exactly, did he want to know about the clown, and what did you tell him?"

"I didn't tell him anything," she said softly. "You know how they were waiting for someone the night I escaped from the cabin and you helped me get away? Well, something he said yesterday brought that memory, too. Al-Jihad was going to use drugs and torture to force me to talk…then Lee was going to kill me, to make sure I never talked again, ever."

"Mariah," he said, his voice soft of the syllables. "What did they ask, exactly?"

"Lee kept wanting to know where the clown was." The memory hurt, constricting her chest and making it hard to breathe. Bearing down on Gray's grip, letting him anchor her as the water thundered around them and the air sparkled with rainbows, she said, "I couldn't tell him. I already ruined their lives once. I couldn't do it again."

Gray exhaled. "Your parents have it."

She nodded, fighting to breathe. "It was my mother's. My father won it for her a long time ago at one of the carnivals they'd worked. I'd always had my eye on it— that one in particular—over all the other little figurines she'd collected. I played with it whenever I could persuade her to let me take it out of its case. She gave it to me the day I left for college, she said so I'd always remember her and my father, and the life I came from. I almost didn't take it, but I knew it was her way of apologizing, if only a little bit, for us not being the best match."

"Believe me, I know how that is," Gray said softly,

and she didn't think he was talking about the case anymore. But then he continued, "How did she end up with the clown?"

"She asked for it." Mariah lifted a shoulder, trying to play it as if she'd understood, though she hadn't really. "Before they moved away, she said she'd like it back, as a reminder of better times. That was why I couldn't tell Lee. He would've gone after her, after both of them." She paused when a terrible thought occurred. "What if he has? Gray, what if—"

"Don't. Mariah, stop!" He shook her, interrupting her building panic. "They're fine, I promise. The FBI does this for a living, remember? We've had a team on your parents since about a half hour after I got you to the city that first night, when we realized you were still involved in this somehow."

"Oh." Mariah blew out a breath, then winced. "Oh. My mother's probably furious with me. If the neighbors find out they're under FBI surveillance and the media circus starts all over again…"

"They'll deal," Gray said firmly. "And so will you." He rose to his feet, drawing her up with him. "First things first, though. We need to have someone pick up that statuette." He paused. "Any idea why your ex wants the clown?"

"Other than to smash it? Not a clue. It's not hollow or anything, so I can't see him hiding something inside it." But there was some logic to the idea. "He could be pretty sure I wouldn't get rid of it, though—he knew it had major sentimental value to me. Which begs the question of why he never did smash it. That's exactly the sort of thing he would've done—something he knew would hurt me, but that he could make into no biggie if I called him on it. 'It was an accident,' he'd say, or, 'I didn't know it meant that much to you.'"

"Since he didn't ruin it," Gray finished for her, "you have to wonder whether he was counting on you keeping it safe…say, for instance, if he spent some time in jail."

"You're right. Come on." Crouching, filling with new purpose, she scooped up her flashlight and headed for the cave entrance. When she didn't hear his footsteps right behind her, she paused and turned back, only to find Gray standing where she'd left him, staring at the waterfall with an odd look on his face. "What is it?"

When he glanced at her, that expression blanked to neutral. "Nothing. Let's go."

But as she led the way back out to the other special agents, and they began the process of contacting Johnson and having an Albuquerque field agent collect her mother's china clown as evidence, Mariah couldn't help thinking that, for the first time since she'd come to know Gray, he'd lied to her.

Whatever he'd been thinking just then, it hadn't been nothing. And he'd been looking at her when he'd thought it.

GRAY SPENT A GOOD half hour on the phone getting Mariah's parents pulled into protective custody over their apparently rather forceful protests, and seizing the ceramic clown from Mrs. Shore. Since she apparently had several dozen of the things and couldn't seem to remember which one she'd gotten back from Mariah, the field agents had bagged and tagged all of them, and were sending them to Bear Claw so Mariah could make a positive ID on the clown in question. So to speak.

Even as the conversation seesawed from deadly serious to mildly ridiculous and back again, Gray was hyperaware of Mariah's position in the cabin relative to his, conscious of her every move and breath. Maybe it was because he'd opened up to her about having lost what he'd practically considered his second family in the bombings; maybe it was the sense that they were finally on to something with this case, and that maybe, just maybe, they were getting close to nailing Mawadi. Whatever the reason, his perceptions of her—and his feelings toward her—had undergone a radical shift.

When he'd awakened by the waterfall and seen her leaning close, he hadn't been thinking of the case or the past as he'd reached up to kiss her. He'd been thinking only of the present. And in that moment, kissing her had been the most important thing in his universe.

She was nothing like the woman he'd thought she was in the first two sets of interviews, nothing like the woman he'd expected to find—or at least spy on—that day nearly a week earlier when he'd hiked up the ridge to the cabin where he was now headquartered, trying to track down a damn china clown her mother had ungifted her.

It might be unfair, but he wasn't getting a very good picture of her parents. His own hadn't been perfect— whose were?—but he'd never once questioned whether he and his sisters were their priority. Even when he'd

disappointed them by splitting with Stacy, his parents
had been on his side. Whatever he needed, they
would've given him if he'd asked. He hadn't, of course.
But it had helped to know that he could. Mariah didn't
have that. As far as he could tell, she'd never had that
from any source, except maybe from her grandfather.

"You still there?" a voice said in his ear, as the agent
he'd been haranguing returned to their telephone conversation, having been scrambling down in the city,
trying to get all the necessary facts.

"Waiting on you," Gray said, though he'd also been
watching through the open bedroom door as Mariah
moved furniture around. Having remembered what her
ex was after, she'd declared herself done with sleeping
in her erstwhile cell. She'd set about turning it back into
a bedroom, at least as much as she could with the deco-
rations and items Mawadi hadn't destroyed. Watching
her, Gray didn't have the heart to tell her they wouldn't
be staying long.

The agent on the other end of the line rattled off the
info Gray had been holding for, which mostly consisted of negatives. No, there hadn't been any evidence
that Mariah's abduction the day before had been a sub-
terfuge designed to distract law enforcement from
another prong of an attack. No, there hadn't been any
indication that al-Jihad had reentered the country, and
there had been no further word on Jane Doe. Everything
was quiet. Too quiet, to Gray's mind. There was an itch
along the center of his spine, a nagging sense that they
were missing something, and it was something that was
going to come back around and bite them, hard.

"And one last thing," the agent said in closing.

"Yes?"

"Johnson said, and I quote, 'Tell him to get his ass down the damn mountain with the woman before all these clowns get here,' end quote." There was a thread of laughter in the guy's voice.

Yeah. Gray had a feeling he was never going to hear the end of the clown thing. "Got it," he said curtly. He signed off and clicked the phone shut, knowing that Mariah wasn't going to like the news.

He couldn't say he was a fan, either, though not for any particular reason he could specify. It was more of a vague disquiet, a sense that they shouldn't make the trip down to the city. But that didn't make any sense, either. He'd never been a cabin-in-the-woods kind of guy. The faint urge to stay another few days, or come back up after all this was over... Those were just situational urges. They'd disappear eventually.

Steeling himself, he joined Mariah in her bedroom, which was already looking more like a room than a jail cell. She'd gotten one of the junior agents to help her move a dresser in from the office, along with an end table and a small desk, and then accessorized with a couple of lamps and the few small pieces of bric-a-brac that had escaped her ex's taste for destruction. The bedclothes were new and she didn't have a rug or curtains, but the room already looked better. More important, at least to him, Mariah looked better. She seemed more settled. Steadier.

He hated having to take that away, to take her away. If it were up to him, he would've stayed the night, and…well, it didn't matter now, did it? "I'm sorry, Mariah," he said gruffly. "We've got to get back down to the city."

She surprised him by nodding. "I figured as much. Your boss will want me to ID the statuette, and probably add me to the protective custody my folks are under. Makes sense to guard us all in one place, right?"

He knew he shouldn't touch her. He did it anyway, a glancing caress on her cheek that brought her head up, brought her eyes to his.

"You're okay with this?" he asked, which was a stupid question, but still. He needed more from her than he was getting. He needed… Hell, he didn't know what he wanted, just that she'd awakened feelings in him that he'd never expected to feel again. She made him want, made him dream. Made him desire, though she was nothing like what he'd thought he wanted.

She met his eyes and laid her hand atop his, capturing his fingers against her cheek. Warmth kindled low in his belly, beside the twist in his gut that wouldn't go away. "I'll be okay," she said. "One of these days, I'll be just fine. And so will you."

"Mariah," he began, but she touched a fingertip to his lips, effectively silencing him.

"Not now," she said softly.

He was grateful she'd stopped him, because he didn't have a damn clue what he'd been about to say. So he went with a lame, "Do you want to pack anything for the trip back down?"

She shook her head. "The terrorists ruined the few things I really cared about."

"Join the club," he said, meaning it to come out light, and wincing when the effort fell flat.

They just stood there for a long moment, staring at one another, and the air hummed with the hard, edgy warmth that always surged through him when they were together, only it was sharper and hotter now, because he knew how she tasted and what she sounded like when she moaned into his mouth. He'd begun to know how her body felt against his, and burned to know more.

He wanted to kiss her, wanted to back her up until she sank down on that wide bed of hers. He wanted to touch every inch of her, worship her, take her. And in doing so, he wanted to give her new memories of the room, of her cabin. He wanted to superimpose his own stamp over the ruin her ex had made of her life. He didn't, though, because he knew, even in the throes of lust, that while he'd be a hell of a lot better for her than her ex had been, he still wasn't what she needed.

She deserved someone who would put her first the way nobody else had done before. She should be the center of someone's universe, the lodestone around which the family revolved. And he knew, deep down inside, that even if Lee, al-Jihad and the others were back behind bars—or dead—and the entire terror network dismantled, he couldn't be that man for her. Not because he didn't want to, but because he simply wasn't capable of it.

Stacy had called him cold and detached, and he was. At first she'd accused him of putting his work ahead of his family. Later, when she'd really stepped back and taken a long, hard look at his relationship with his parents, she'd changed that to encompass putting his work ahead of her, and she'd been right. He'd been so determined to find a perfect match, as his parents had—finding a woman from a cop family, one who would get what it meant to be married to a cop—that he hadn't stopped to really think about why his parents' marriage had worked. It wasn't because of the job or how his mother handled things. It was because his parents loved each other. Somehow Gray had lost track of that feeling, of how to find and keep it. He'd thought he loved Stacy, but really she'd simply been a good fit, or what he'd thought was a good fit. And he'd thought he'd loved Ken and Trish, and especially baby Catherine. But if that were the case, why hadn't he managed to catch and put away their killers by now?

Instead, here he was, on the verge of losing his job and obsessed with a woman who was more wrong for him than Stacy had ever been.

But knowing it, knowing how wrong he and Mariah were on paper, even though for some reason they seemed to click in person, he let his hand drop and stepped away. "Then if you're ready, we should get going."

She looked at him long and hard before she nodded. "I'm ready."

She headed for the door without hesitating, without looking back, and Gray got the distinct impression that they'd just agreed to far more than driving back down to the city. He was pretty sure they'd just agreed that it—whatever *it* had been starting to happen between them—was over.

Logic said he should be relieved.

Logic could go to hell.

"Mariah, wait," he said, taking two long strides to catch up to her. "Wait. I think we need to—"

He didn't get a chance to finish his thought, because at that moment the sound of gunfire erupted from the front of the cabin, there was a *whump* of detonation, and the world exploded around him.

# Chapter Nine

Mariah screamed as the flames engulfed the front room of the cabin. This wasn't happening, she told herself. This couldn't be happening. Only it could and it was.

"This way." Gray grabbed her arm with one hand, his weapon appearing in the other, held with deadly intent. "Out the back."

She started to follow him, then dug in her heels when she heard the crack of gunfire from out front, followed by a cry of pain. "Shouldn't we—"

"No," he said flatly. "We shouldn't. Right now, you're more important than they are." It was the soldier talking now, not the man, but she could tell that it cost him.

Another explosion detonated outside, and when she glanced through a window, she saw the two FBI vehicles in flames.

This time when Gray yanked at her, urging her out the back, she followed without protest, scrambling, stumbling, clinging to him because he was the one sure, solid thing she knew she could hang on to in the midst of chaos.

He stopped at the back door, took a look around the partially cleared office, grabbed a couple of lamps and set them near the door. Then he moved to a ruined coffee table, with two of four legs broken—Lee's handiwork. Made of hardwood, the tabletop was criss-crossed with rusted iron strapping and impregnated with old hand-forged nails, mute testimony that the wood had been reclaimed from one of the local mills.

Using the remaining two legs as handles, Gray lifted the flat wooden slab and nodded with grim satisfaction. "It'll do."

Mariah didn't have to ask for what, because she could guess—as a shield. They had to assume that Lee and the others had the rear exit covered.

Gray glanced back at her, his eyes steely with determination and rage. "Ready?"

*No.* "Yes."

"Let's go. Keep your head down and *move!*"

He kicked open the door and hurled the lamps out. Gunfire spat from the tree line, coming from two positions, one dead ahead of them, the other slightly to the right.

Holding up their makeshift shield, Gray rushed out the door. Mariah followed and got in the lee of the slab, ducking to stay below the protected level and keeping her feet moving. Gray angled them to the left, away from where the gunfire had come, and charged for the forest.

Grabbing an edge of the table, partly to help and partly to keep herself steady as they hurdled over the stumps she'd clear-cut for her own protection, Mariah ran for her life.

Gunfire chattered and bullets slammed into the heavy wood of the table, some of them pinging as they ricocheted off the embedded metal. A new, larger explosion ripped through the air, and heat scorched her skin.

She didn't look back, didn't need to. Lee had left the cabin standing as bait of his own, knowing how important her home was to her. Now, if he couldn't trap or kill her in it, he would destroy it, knowing how much the loss would hurt.

"No!" she screamed, denying the evil that she'd married.

"Are you hit?" Gray shouted, not looking back as he maneuvered them closer to the trees, shifting his grip to fire a few rounds off to their left, though she didn't know if he'd seen someone or was laying cover fire.

"No, I'm mad. Get us out of here so we can nail these bastards!" That was all that drove her now—less fear for her own safety and more the knowledge that she had to stay alive long enough to identify the statuette and help Gray and his people figure out why Lee had wanted the thing. For the first time, she thought she understood why and how Gray had subsumed his own life and needs for so long beneath the mantle of revenge. She only hoped she lived long enough to do the same.

Gunfire erupted from their unprotected side as they hit the tree line, stitching a line of bullet strikes in the forest floor just as the continued barrage from the other side finally took its toll on the wooden slab, which all but crumbled under the onslaught.

Tossing the tabletop, Gray grabbed Mariah's hand. "Come on!"

Together, they bolted into the woods.

Déjà vu ripped through her, and she had a crazy moment of profound gratitude that she was at least wearing shoes this time, and hadn't spent the previous five days tied to her own bed, drugged and disoriented.

Then again, she also wasn't trying to elude only two men. From the amount of chaos coming from the front of the cabin, where her Jeep and the other vehicles burned, smudging the air with choking smoke and the roar of fire, she knew Lee had come with a team. And, unlike Brisbane, it didn't seem as though they had any compunction about killing her this time.

So, clinging to Gray's hand as her only anchor in a storm of gunfire and insanity, she ran as hard and fast as she could.

Moments later came the sounds of pursuit, and a familiar voice shouting, "Get her! No, go around that way!"

At Gray's glance, she nodded and confirmed, "Lee."

He cursed as the sounds of pursuit intensified. "The others couldn't hold them."

She didn't ask if that meant the agents were dead; she didn't want to know just then. She could feel the guilt later. Right now, she and Gray needed to get out of there and back down to the city.

Realizing that they were running uphill, not down, she said, fitting the words between breaths as she began to labor with the effort, "Should we circle back to the cars?"

"The cars are gone," he reminded her. "What's up this way?"

"Trees."

"Damn."

Back when she'd bought the cabin, its isolation had been a blessing, its location suitable for her self-imposed penance. Now, she found herself wishing that she'd bought a condo in the city, where screaming for help might've gotten her somewhere.

"Let's stop here for a second." Gray pulled her into the lee of a big, lichen-covered boulder, then leaned back against it, breathing hard. "Quiet. I think they've stopped."

They strained to regulate their breathing, listening intently. Mariah could all but picture Lee and his men doing the same thing.

There was only silence. Either Lee and the others had stopped as well, they'd retreated…or they were creeping up on the boulder, soundlessly, aiming to surround her and Gray and gun them down where they stood. That thought brought a huge shiver crawling down Mariah's back, and she unconsciously moved closer to the man who, thus far, had consistently chosen retreat over attack in an effort to keep her safe, despite his claims that he'd turn her over if it meant he'd get justice for his friends and the others.

She was vaguely surprised when Gray curled an arm around her and hugged her to his side. "I've got you," he whispered, not looking at her, but instead scanning the forest around them.

*Yes,* a small voice whispered inside her, *but who's got you?* He stood alone so often, apart from his so-called teammates. His boss didn't like him; his wife had divorced him; he didn't speak about his family; he felt responsible for the deaths of his closest friends; and his only living friend that she knew of, Jonah Fairfax, was engaged to be married to a special agent-in-training and was off on a vendetta of his own, trying to track down his former boss, agent-turned-traitor Jane Doe.

For a man Mariah had initially thought of as just another cog in the FBI machine that seemed determined to tear her life and family apart, Gray had turned out to be as much of a loner as she was, if not more so, with one main difference: she sought solitude, while he carried his with him.

When there was no sound or movement from the direction of the cabin, Gray eased his arm from around Mariah to dig into his pocket and pull out his long-range cell phone. "Hopefully, one of the other agents got off a mayday and reinforcements are already on their way up." He punched a speed-dial button, then held the phone to his ear. "Won't hurt to follow up, though. Johnson should be able to get a chopper up here."

There were too many *hopefullys* and *ifs* in that statement, Mariah knew. Her fear was confirmed when Gray cursed, stabbed a couple more buttons on the phone, then flipped it shut and shoved it back into his pocket.

"What's wrong?"

"Signal's jammed."

He didn't give her time to process that, or what it might mean. Instead, he pushed away from the boulder and held out a hand. "Come on, we need to—" He broke off when a new sound encroached on the silence: the low thump of helicopter rotors.

"Yours?" Mariah asked hopefully. Was their rescue at hand so quickly?

"Maybe." But he didn't sound optimistic. He glanced at her, and there was worry in his gray eyes. "The timing doesn't quite mesh, unless Johnson had the bird on its way up the ridge already, which he wouldn't have had any reason to do."

A chill settled into her bones. "Then it's al-Jihad's."

"Could be." He took her hand and tugged her along. "Could just be sightseers or flight lessons."

"All the way out here?"

"Yeah. Not likely. And if they're coming after us, we have to assume they're prepared for a forest search this time—infrared, night vision, the works." He took a long look around at their surroundings. "It'll be dark soon, and there's no way we can chance looping back around to the cabin. Better to hole up for the night and try to get to cell range in the morning." He paused. "How far are we from that cave of yours?"

Determined not to panic, not to despair, Mariah took a good look around, followed by a glance at the setting sun, and forced her voice to sound level. "A mile, maybe more. I'm pretty sure there's a river between here and there. It's fordable, but we'll get wet."

"We'll have to chance it," he decided. "The water could be to our benefit if they bring in tracking dogs."

She shivered at the thought. It seemed unbelievable that this could be happening. Less than an hour earlier she'd been under full FBI protection. Now she and Gray were cut off and on their own. "Won't your boss figure out that something's wrong when you guys don't check in on schedule?"

"Of course, but depending on what's going on with the case, he might send a single car up to see if our communications went down, rather than sending in the cavalry right away. That'll take time." Gray lifted a hand and touched her cheek in a gesture that was more reassuring than sensual, though there was heat there, as well. "Can you take me back to your cave?"

She hesitated as something deep inside her warned that that was a bad idea, that too much had changed too quickly between them, but what other choice did she have? His logic was irrefutable; they needed someplace safe to hide for the night. She didn't know anyplace better than the cave system leading to the secret waterfall. Dammit.

Hating the thought of bringing fear and uncertainty into her small zone of peace, hating that Lee was taking that from her, too, she nodded and firmed her chin. "Follow me."

She led the way and he fell in behind her, each of them straining to hear the sounds of pursuit. The chopper noise passed over them and faded, but Mariah knew that was no guarantee either way. Maybe the terrorists were conferring over search plans. Maybe the agents had gotten a message through and reinforcements had already arrived at the burning cabin. They just didn't know, and couldn't risk going back to take a look.

For now, hiding was her and Gray's best and only option. Tomorrow, they'd find some way to fight back, or die trying.

IT TOOK THEM NEARLY an hour to reach the cave. The river crossing was shallow, but the water current was stronger than Gray would've liked, the flow tugging halfway up his thighs as they fought their way upriver, working to confuse trackers. They were most of the way to where Mariah had indicated they should climb out, when the chopper's rotor thump returned.

Without a word, working in the strange synchrony that kept developing between them when he least expected it, they both dropped down into the water, submerging themselves almost completely.

The cold water killed their heat signatures instantly, and the helicopter passed overhead without incident. In the last of the fading light, Gray looked up at the passing bird and got a glimpse of a sleek-nosed shape with regulation FAA tail numbers but no official seal. Not FBI, then. Maybe rented, maybe private. Almost certainly al-Jihad.

When the helicopter had moved on, he and Mariah dragged themselves to the riverbank, and up and out of the water, shivering. The night air cut quickly through their wet clothing, making the chill even worse.

"We need to get moving," he said, the words coming out shaky as his jaw chattered.

She nodded, but didn't speak, and she didn't protest when he took her hand and walked at her side rather than bringing up the rear guard. Helping each other, leaning into one another for warmth, they staggered onward. By the time they crawled up the rock face leading to the hidden ledge, it was fully dark and he was all but carrying her, with his arm looped around her waist, hers around his neck. She was shivering and in shock, but she hadn't complained, hadn't given up.

The moon was out, which was a damn good thing, since they didn't have even her small flashlight. When they got inside the cave, he lit the way with his cell phone—stupid thing couldn't call out, but at least it was water-resistant enough that it was still working, and the display light was good for something.

His initial intention had been for them to spend the night in the cave itself, but the dip in the river had changed the direction of his thoughts. They needed to get warm. In the absence of matches, a lighter or any certainty that either of them could start a fire from scratch, and not being sure a campfire was the best idea, even inside the cave, his next best choice was to keep going, all the way to the hidden glen with its strangely warm water.

"Will the pool be warm enough to camouflage us if they fly over?" Mariah asked softly. She'd all but stopped trembling, which was a bad sign, indicating that her body was starting to shut down on her.

The real answer to her question was "We don't have a choice," followed by "If it's warm enough to hide us, it's warm enough to show up on infrared, which could mean they might give it a second or third look." But Gray knew she needed more from him than that, so he said, "Absolutely." And, as they neared the smaller offshoot that would lead them to the hidden canyon, he hoped it wasn't a lie.

"Wait here. I'll be right back." Mariah paused, took the phone and moved away from him, stumbling a little as she walked deeper into the main branch of the cave. Gray did as she'd ordered, but he tracked her progress by the glow of the phone and the small sounds she made, and held himself ready to go after her, if necessary.

He heard the sound of rock shifting against rock, and called out, "What's going on over there? You have this place outfitted with a secret door that leads straight back to the city?"

"Not quite that good, but I think it'll help." She returned, carrying his phone in one hand and a battered, dusty canvas knapsack in the other. "I built a cairn a little farther in and stashed some emergency supplies in case…well, just in case. We've got some energy bars, water, a blanket and a first aid kit. Not exactly the comforts of home, but it'll help."

"Any matches?"

"Yeah, but they're soaked. One of the water bottles leaked."

"Bummer," Gray said, but felt something ease in his chest when she rejoined him. At the same time, something else tightened within him.

This wasn't just the place she'd come for peace, he realized. It had also been her bolt-hole. If she were outside the cabin's perimeter when the alarms sounded, she'd intended to come here and hide. The knowledge wasn't surprising; she'd proven herself a survivor time and again.

What was surprising was the hard squeeze that caught him beneath his heart, and the sadness that accompanied it.

The system had failed her so badly that she'd felt the need to protect herself in isolation. Worse, he'd been part of that system. In the process of trying to save the world from the terrorists' threat and gain justice for Ken and his family, Gray had lost sight of some of the other people involved. He'd seen Mariah alternately as an asset or an obstacle. He'd forgotten to remember that she was also one of the innocents he was charged with protecting.

In the blue-white light from the cell phone, her expression shifted to one of worry. "What's wrong?"

"I'm sorry." He took the knapsack from her, let her keep the phone for the dim glow it provided.

She frowned. "For anything in particular?"

For most of it, he realized. He was sorry for how he'd treated her and her family during the first round of the investigation; sorry that al-Jihad and his conspirators had outsmarted some of the country's best and brightest to escape from the ARX Supermax; sorry that once they had, she'd been treated with more suspicion than compassion, and hadn't felt safe in her own home. Hell, she hadn't *been* safe in her own home, and even once she'd gotten free, Gray had turned around and put her right back in harm's way. It didn't matter that she'd volunteered to become bait, he should've been man enough, agent enough, to say *no thanks* and tuck her into protective custody, far away from Bear Claw City. Instead, he'd used her and nearly gotten her killed. More than that, he'd kissed her. He'd known she was growing attached to him and hadn't done anything about it.

But he was too much of a coward to tell her that, so he focused on the matter at hand, on the failure of the system. "I'm sorry the FBI wasn't there for you, and that you figured you were better off alone than under our protection."

Her expression flattened to something he couldn't quite interpret, but she said only, "Come on. I'm freezing."

He ducked and followed her through the narrower offshoot cave, breathing a sigh of relief when they emerged once again out into the open.

The air warmed palpably, and the hidden valley spread out beneath them, the waterfall close enough to touch. Moonlight bathed the scene, a magnificent display of blue-white light that sparkled on the plunging waterfall and the rioting surface of the pool below, all of it cast over by the mist, which had thickened as the night air cooled.

Gray paused, awestruck by the beauty of the scene. But he knew there were more practical, immediate issues to deal with. They needed to get warm, and quickly.

"Come on." He holstered his weapon, which by his count had a scant four or five rounds left in it, shifted the bulky knapsack onto his shoulder and held out a hand to Mariah.

They helped each other down the narrow path to the flat rock, which was damp and slippery with condensation, and shrouded in mist. The moist air beaded on Gray's hands and face, and the contrast between the warmth of the stone and the damp chill of his clothes made him long for the hot, dry warmth of a fire.

The thought made him flash on his last sight of Mariah's cabin. He'd looked back as they had fled, and had seen flames licking from the front of the log structure, devouring the porch.

He wanted to believe that the other agents had gotten to safety, that the gunfire they'd heard had been a rearguard action, but he feared that wasn't the case. The cabin was gone. His backup was gone. And Lee and the others were on the hunt.

The terrorists had torched the cabin, indicating that they knew full well that the statuette wasn't there. But was that because Lee had searched the place top to bottom while he'd been in residence…or was it because someone privy to the investigation itself had leaked information on the great clown roundup down in Albuquerque? If the latter, what did it mean in terms of the FBI's response when the ridgeline team failed to check in at midnight? Would a conspirator within Johnson's group try to delay their rescue?

"Hey," Mariah said, breaking into his reverie. "Turn it off for a little bit. Right now we need to concentrate on getting warm, having a snack, maybe scouting one of the other caves as an escape route and then bunking down as safely as possible. There's nothing more we can do until daylight."

"Yeah. I know." But he shook his head. "This wasn't how it was supposed to happen, you know?"

"Story of my life." She dropped his hand, and, with her eyes on his, took a couple of steps back until she was all but obscured by the mist. "I'm serious, though. I think we should turn it off and think of something else."

It wasn't until he heard the plop of wet cloth hitting the rock ledge that he realized he was staring at her.

"Mariah," he said, the word coming out on a soft growl. "What are you doing?"

"My clothes are soaked. I'm taking them off and hanging them off the backside of the rock in hopes that they'll dry a little while I'm hot-tubbing it, so to speak." The practicality of the response was somewhat undercut by the faint tremor in her voice, one that spoke more of nerves than chill, and turned her tone husky when she said, "I think you should do the same."

He wanted to, more than he'd wanted to do just about anything else, ever. But hadn't he just been thinking of all the things he'd done wrong when it came to her? He didn't think he could add "took advantage of her at a particularly vulnerable time" to the list and still look himself in the eye afterward.

Though a large part of him wanted to do just that, and damn the consequences.

Keeping his voice gentle when it wanted to go rough, he said, "You've had a hell of a day, on top of a hell of a week. Don't do something you'll regret later on, when all this is over and we go back to our normal lives."

He thought the corners of her mouth turned up in a small, sad smile, though he couldn't be sure in the moonlight and mist. "What's normal? My cabin is gone. Even if part of it is salvageable, I won't be able to live there by myself again and feel safe. Even if

Lee's out of the picture, how will I know that another one of al-Jihad's men won't come after me?"

There it was again, her basic, well-earned distrust of the system. Gray wanted to tell her to have some faith, but who was he to talk?

Half the time he went around his boss, trying to do what he thought was best. In that, he and Mariah weren't so different. They were very different in all the other ways that mattered, though. Or, rather, they were too alike to be compatible—both hardheaded and stubborn, and too used to fixing their own problems rather than working as part of a team. Which by all rational interpretations of right and wrong meant he should turn away while she finished undressing and slipped beneath the surface of the swirling pool.

But he didn't.

He kept watching as she shimmied out of her shirt and panties, and unhooked her bra, each motion camouflaged by the mist, letting him see impressions but not details, lending romance to something that should have been simple expediency, but had become something more.

"You'll get through this," he said with quiet certainty, even as his blood heated and his heart set an increasing tempo. "You're going to get through this and come out the other side, and you're going to make the life you want. Maybe you'll make up with your parents, maybe not. Maybe you'll rebuild the cabin, maybe not. You'll make those choices for yourself, not anyone else, and you'll figure out what comes next. I have faith in that, in you, and I'm not a man who's big on faith."

This time her smile was more genuine. "Yeah. That

much I've figured out." She let the bra dangle from her fingertips, then drop to the stone surface. She took one step toward him. Then another.

Gray's breath caught at the moonlight-limned sight of her. He drew his eyes from her gracefully muscled calves up the long, curving sweep of her thighs and hips, along the dip of her waist to the symmetrical globes of her breasts, which were tipped with dark, pouting aureolas and nipples that puckered in the warm moist air, crinkling under his regard.

"Mariah," he said again, this time not in warning but almost as a plea.

*Don't ask me to do this,* one part of him wanted to say, while another, equally strong part wanted to say, *Don't stop, come closer, let me touch you.*

"Gray," she said in answer, stopping very close to him, so her eyes dominated his vision and his breath came thin in his lungs. "Don't worry, I don't think this is love, or even the beginning of something that will last beyond tonight. But over the past few days, I've had good reason to take stock of my life. I've thought about the things I'd regret doing, and regret *not* doing, if Lee gets me before you get him."

Her words were matter-of-fact, and they brought a deathly chill to his gut. "I won't let that happen."

"Maybe you should." She held up a hand when he started to argue. "I'm not saying I want to die—absolutely not. But you said it yourself—there might come a time when saving me might mean letting him go. If that happens, I hope you'll do the right thing."

"I will," he said, his voice harsh. "I'll get you the hell

out of there and stick you in protective custody where you should've been all along. Then I'll get a team back out there, and go after the bastard."

"And what will he have done in the meantime?" Her eyes were sad, but resolute. "How many people died in the bombings? How many would've died if al-Jihad's plan to destroy the stadium hadn't been foiled?"

"But it was."

"We might not be so lucky the next time, and you know it. Tell me I'm wrong."

He wanted to grab her and shake some sense into her. He wanted to protect her, to kiss her, to make love to her, to throw his head back and shout at the moon, railing against the unfairness of it, the cruelty of men who destroyed for nothing more than their own pleasure, though they might disguise it as something else. Men like her ex and al-Jihad.

"Tell me," she pressed.

"You're not wrong," he admitted, though the words laid him bare.

"Then knowing that, knowing what you might have to do in the next couple of days, tell me you'll do me a favor."

"What favor?"

"I don't want my biggest regret to be that Lee was my first and only lover."

Shock rattled through Gray, followed by understanding and a sharp twist of grief for the purity that an evil man had used for his own purposes. "Mariah," he said, voice catching in his throat, "no." He wasn't sure if he was denying her words or the greedy leap inside him, the one that wanted her, that would take her on the thinnest of excuses.

She lifted a shoulder in a half shrug, and though her eyes were full of uncertainty, there was only acceptance in her voice when she said, "Your call, Gray. If the answer is no, your reasons are your own, and I'll respect them, as I've come to respect you." She touched her lips to his, bringing a spike of heat and a thrill of passion to the complicated mix of emotions that tangled together inside him. "Just as I'll still respect you if you say yes."

Her lips left his as she backed off a few steps. Then she turned, dove cleanly into the warm water and was gone, leaving him standing on the stone overlook, trying to figure out what had just happened to turn his world inside out. And what the hell he was going to do, when what he wanted to do conflicted so thoroughly with what he knew was right.

# Chapter Ten

Mariah told herself she was trembling because of the cold, but even her conscious mind knew that was a crock. She was wired tight, her body humming with nerves as her immediate future hung balanced on the knifepoint of Gray's choice.

She held her breath, hovering beneath the churning water, which warmed her flesh as she tried to guess what he would decide. Would she surface to see him sitting cross-legged at the edge of the stone ledge, watching over her as she bathed, protector but not lover? Or was he even now stripping down to the hard body she'd felt beneath his clothing, preparing to dive into the pool naked, in tacit agreement with her plan?

She stayed under as long as she could, unwilling to surface and learn the answer. She wanted this, wanted him, for all the reasons she'd cited, and because she'd done the wrong thing before in choosing a man who'd seemed so right for her. This time, she was picking one she knew was wrong, and going in with her eyes wide open.

Knowing that even making the choice was part of

taking control back from the memory of what Lee had done to her, she rose and broke the surface, sucking in a deep breath of air.

She nearly got a lungful of water as Gray dove in beside her.

The impact of his body rocked the churning waters that surrounded her and brought a flare of heat to her belly, a balm of healing to her soul. They might be wrong for each other, she knew, but in this moment they were exactly right.

He surfaced a few feet away from her, treading water as he smoothed back his short-cut hair, leaving it bristling on end, dark in the silver-blue moonlight. He didn't speak as he sculled toward her, gliding across the distance that separated them.

As he did so, Mariah was acutely aware of the warm press of water on her suddenly sensitized skin. No longer chilled, she burned from within and reveled in the sly touch of watery currents. Mist surrounded them, bringing clinging wetness with every breath, and when she licked her lips, the moisture carried a tang of minerals and a thrill of excitement.

She skimmed gently backward, until she was standing on a submerged outcropping, the water lapping at her collarbones. Gray followed and stopped very near her, not touching her, but close enough that she could touch him if she reached out.

When he didn't say or do anything, just looked at her, his eyes serious and silver in the moonlight, she said, "I wasn't sure you'd agree to this." She rushed on before he interrupted, "I know we said we couldn't—

and shouldn't—do this, but I'm not suggesting that we start something. I just want a new memory—one that's true, rather than tainted." She looked up into the sky, letting her head tip back and her hair dip into the blood-warm water as mist feathered her face like the faintest of kisses. "I want to make love, here under the waterfall, in a place that's brought me peace. And don't worry—I'm using the word *love* in its most generic sense. I want to love life, love our bodies, love what I feel when I'm near you." She straightened to look at him once again. "Did I just scare the hell out of you?"

"No," he said simply. "You've humbled me. And you make me wish I were a better man, one who could let this be the start of something, rather than just a memory." He paused, looking around as she had done moments earlier. "You make me wish I had flowers to give you, or poetry. Something worthy of this place and what we're about to do in it. But I'm not a romantic and I haven't got a way with words, so I'll just say it plainly. This will be a memory for me, too, Mariah. I haven't been with another woman since Stacy. I haven't wanted anyone that way. Then I saw you."

Mariah thought she felt her heart sigh, and maybe break and bleed a little for what she couldn't have. But this was her deal, her terms, so she said only, "I wasn't looking for poetry or romance, but you just gave me enough of both to count as a memory in itself."

There was beauty, too, in the powerful promise of his bare shoulders, the bulge of his biceps and the glistening planes of his upper torso. There was poetry there, whether he knew it or not.

They drew together and kissed then, because it was impossible not to. The attraction that had started as sparks and grown into something more flared from a warm kernel in Mariah's belly to a lick of heat when his lips touched hers.

That was the only point of contact at first—mouth on mouth. Mariah tasted the tang of mineralized water on his lips, and gloried in the press of wetness, of heat. She felt the brush of his bare legs against hers, felt one of his hands skim across her hip.

A bubble of joy burst through her at the caress, and the glint that entered his eyes. His normally closed expression held acceptance, anticipation and blatant male hunger. She touched her lips to his, then sank into the kiss, into the water, and tangled her legs with his. They dipped beneath the surface, lost in each other.

The kiss spun out on a single breath, a single moment, as they came together, skin on skin, with her breasts pressed against his powerfully sculpted chest, and the solid, hard length of his erection nestled between them. Her flesh burned at the points of contact, and the perfection of the fit, the feeling of connectedness, was so acute she shied away from it, afraid she was in over her head, figuratively as well as literally.

With a powerful surge, he sent them back to the surface. Mariah's head was spinning when they broke into the misty air, and she regained her footing. She ended the kiss to suck in a great lungful of air, exhaling it again on a delighted laugh when Gray hooked an arm around her, pulled her from the ledge and started swimming, aiming them at the waterfall.

"You'll drown us!" she exclaimed, though she hung on to his neck, reveling in the coarse friction of masculine hair against her water-softened skin, and the powerful play of muscles as he drew them beneath the thundering stream.

"Then you'd better hang on!" With that scant warning, he dove beneath the waterfall, wrapping his arms around her and taking her with him.

They surfaced, laughing, in the sheltered space behind the waterfall. She'd swum there before, and had explored the small niche where centuries—maybe millennia—of watery friction had carved a soft-edged bowl in the stones behind the cataract. She'd never been there at night, though, never seen it moonlit.

"Oh," she said in a small gasp of pleasure as Gray released her, touched bottom and stood, rising over her to inspect the ledge.

The silvery moonlight cast the waterfall in a brilliant white glow. Against it, Gray was a black silhouette of masculinity as he reached down to take her hand. "Come here," he said, his voice pitched low beneath the waterfall's thunder.

Mariah went. How could she not join him in the shallow niche? How could she not rise from the water with him, and lie with him there, in that place outside reality?

They lay on their sides on the warm, water-smoothed stone, facing each other, and sank into a kiss that spun out endlessly. The water cooled slightly on Mariah's skin, bringing delicious shivers instead of chills as she touched him, tentatively at first, running her hands over his shoulders and down the leashed strength of his arms.

He copied her actions, slicking the water on her skin and kindling the sparks within her to a flame. She murmured her pleasure and crowded close.

It was all that she'd dreamed of in her premarriage fantasies—a romantic setting with a handsome man, out in the open, though with little threat of discovery. The realization brought a laugh bubbling to the surface, and Gray pulled away to look down at her, his features unreadable in the dark silhouette of his powerful form.

"That tickle?"

"No. Or rather, yes, but in a good way." She paused, then went with the truth. "I was just thinking that before—well, when I was younger—I always imagined doing this outside. I never have until now."

A low growl rumbled in his chest, a mix of amusement and feral sexuality that kicked her pulse a notch higher. "What, exactly, did you imagine?"

She blushed hard and hot. And she told him, embellishing in the places where her innocence had fallen short before marriage. Not that her marital sex had been great, ranging as it had along a descending continuum from pleasant to domineering, but it had given her some ideas of how things were supposed to work.

And oh, boy, did they. Gray took her at her word and then went from there, kissing her, touching her, exploring her body more intimately than she'd imagined in the not-so-wild fantasies that had suddenly become real, and then been exceeded. He licked her, suckled her, made her bow back in ecstasy.

A small orgasm caught her unexpectedly, vising her inner muscles in a long, languid pull of pleasure that had her crying out, her words lost beneath the water-thunder. Then he was shifting onto his back, and lifting her above him.

She stiffened. "I don't know—"

"The stone's worn smooth, but it's still stone. Trust me, this'll work better than me squashing you flat. And…it'll let you work out more of those fantasies. That is, assuming you've had a few of what you'd like to do to your lover."

She didn't miss his use of the generic—he hadn't said "what you'd like to do to me," as though any man would've done once she'd made the decision to take a lover. Though she understood his need for distance, she put a purr in her voice when she said, "I don't know about that, but I've definitely gotten a few ideas over the past week or so."

And she proceeded to show him.

If she fumbled anything, he didn't seem to notice or care, showing her his appreciation with long, possessive strokes down her back and sides, letting her hear it in his groans. When it finally became too much, when they'd driven each other beyond reason and joining wasn't just the next step, it was the only one, he gripped her hips in his powerful hands and shifted her so the long, hard length of his erection was poised for entry.

There, he paused. "Okay?" he asked, his voice a sexy rumble almost the same pitch as the water. "We're condomless, but I'm clean."

"Oh." Positioned there, poised for the most intimate

of joinings, she scrambled to collect her thoughts. "Yeah. Yeah, we're good. I got tested after…well, after." After she learned her husband wasn't even close to being the man she'd thought. "As far as the other, I've got an IUD. For medical reasons, not because I sleep around."

"Yeah. I sort of got that from the part where you haven't been with anyone except the ex."

The reminder probably should've been a cold one. Instead, it made the comparison between the two men that much more poignant.

Lee had insisted on being on top, on being in control. Gray had touched her the way she wanted, then put himself on the bottom so he'd be the one with his back to the stone.

Because of that, she found a smile when part of her wanted to weep for the girl she'd been, for the way her life might've gone if she'd chosen better the first time around. "Then that's your answer. Bombs away."

Her words were flip, but there was nothing frivolous about the sensations or emotions when she eased down and back, taking him within her. She couldn't see his face in the darkness behind the waterfall, but she could feel his intensity in the reverence of his touch, hear it in the catch of his breath and his low hiss of pleasure.

He was large inside her, filling her, stretching her, his size magnifying each sensation, every burst of pleasure. Her eyelids eased down, blocking out even the silver glow of moonlight. The sound of the waterfall surrounded her, as did the feel of the man who moved beneath her, urging her, guiding her, touching her as he whispered praise and promises, making her feel every bit of the woman she'd once imagined herself becoming.

She bent to kiss him and he rose to meet her, so they were sitting face-to-face, with her straddling his lap. The position brought new sensations, new heats and desires. She went with them, riding him until they were both groaning and gasping and laughing, partners in pleasure.

Then he dropped them down into the water, still joined, still wrapped together. He pressed her back against the stone wall, pinning her hips in place and driving deep.

Mariah arched back on a strangled gasp, gripping his shoulders as the sensations within her changed from pleasure to blinding heat, from play to something larger and darker, an all-consuming need that threatened to take over and leave her helpless.

Yet even as Gray thrust into her, pressing her against the stone and holding her steady as he pistoned, she knew he was as much in her power as she was in his. This pleasure was a give-and-take, not a domination.

The knowledge, and the strength it brought, gave her the confidence to let go. She strained into him, against him, and touched her lips to his.

The kiss held a sweetness at odds with the rampaging fury of their bodies. She sank into it, into him, and heard him murmur her name as the awesome madness of their pleasure rose up, sweeping her into a pulsing coil of heat and need, and the power they made together.

Her orgasm was a long, throbbing pull of pleasure that bound her to him, and him to her, as he shuddered in her arms and cut loose. She felt him surge within her, felt her inner muscles contract to prolong the spasms—his, hers, theirs. And when she leaned back onto the rock ledge where he'd held her pinned, he followed her down, turning them so they were on their sides, she tucked against him. Then he turned his face into the side of her neck, breathing her in. And whispered her name once again.

GRAY'S WORLD HAD GONE soft and warm, smoothing out all the edges he'd lived with for so long. Mariah was curled up against him, her back to his front and his hands folded with hers beneath her chin.

Yet, at the same time, she surrounded him as surely as the warm mists and the water that ran from their bodies. He breathed her in, felt her in every cell of his body. He'd just spent himself inside her, yet he wanted her again already. He'd been her first lover in all the ways that mattered, the first to be with her for her own sake, and his, not because of some nefarious plan.

The thought of Lee and al-Jihad brought too much reality into a moment where it didn't belong, so Gray pushed the outside world aside and touched his lips to Mariah's neck, kissing the soft place behind her ear. She shuddered against him, raised their joined hands to her lips, and pressed a kiss into the center of his palm.

The simple gesture, one of love and acceptance, sent a poignant jolt through his system, and a whispered thought: *I wish.* He wished he were a better man with a different life. He wished he could offer her a home and a lifetime. Those wishes were so strong, yet so incompatible with the things that had driven him for so long. And still, part of him said, *What if?*

What if he put aside his drive for revenge and made a new life for himself? For them? He could turn in his gun and badge; they could rebuild the cabin, and then…

And then what? He was a cop from a family of cops. He knew policework, loved it. He didn't have any hobbies, didn't know who or what he'd be without the job. More than that, there were Ken, Trish and Catherine, and all the others al-Jihad and his men had killed. They no longer had their lives or loves. Didn't he owe it to them to put off his own until justice was served?

Still, he wished. And because he wished, because the desire to make an impossible change was so strong that it nearly consumed him, he eased away from her. "We should swim back out and check the phone. If Lee and the others have left the vicinity, they may have taken the signal scrambler with them." When that came out more coolly practical than he'd meant it to, he consciously softened his tone. "Besides, I could do with one of those energy bars. You just about used me up."

She lay still for a moment, then rolled away from him and sat up, her gloriously naked female form silhouetted against the silver rain. He couldn't see her expression, but her voice was carefully neutral when she said, "Back to reality, then?"

"Back to reality." When that seemed pitifully inadequate, especially considering the undeniable depth of what had just happened between them, he tried to explain. "It's not that—"

"Don't," she said, interrupting with the single, soft word. "Please, don't. I didn't mean for this to complicate things. I just…I wanted a better memory. Which is exactly what you've given me."

"What if I want more than that?" he said. He should've been shocked by his own words. Instead, they felt exactly right.

"Do you?"

"Maybe."

She shifted, and a glint of refracted moonlight allowed him to see her small, sad smile. "Even if that 'maybe' had been a heartfelt 'yes,' my answer would be that I'm flattered, but we both know I'd need and want more from you than you're willing to give." She paused, and when he didn't argue, she nodded. "Yeah. Thought so."

"If it helps at all, I wish things were different."

"But not enough to change them."

Something squeezed tight in his chest. "I can't."

She nodded. "Then there we are." She leaned into him and touched her lips to his, surprising him. The heat gathered, sparked higher. But then she eased back, with that same sad smile in place. "Goodbye, Gray."

Neither of them was going anywhere at that moment, but he knew what she meant, knew that this was the end of anything physical between them, which was something they probably shouldn't have started, but he'd be damned if he'd regret it. She wasn't the only one who'd made new memories just now.

He tipped his head in acknowledgment. "Goodbye, Mariah. And good luck."

Together, they slipped into the warm mineral waters,

ducked beneath the waterfall and swam to the flat boulder where they'd left their clothes and supplies. They dressed in awkward silence and she rummaged through her dusty pack for food and water while he checked his phone.

The signal was good, and a text awaited him: *Tracking your GPS; chopper ETA 30 min.* The time stamp said they were down to less than ten minutes.

He showed the message to Mariah, who smiled sadly as water dripped from her hair like tears. "Well, then. Back to reality it is."

"Yeah," Gray said, and turned away, gritting his teeth at the sudden realization that he damn well didn't want to go back to reality. He wanted to stay exactly where he was.

THE PICKUP WENT SMOOTHLY, with no sign of Lee or al-Jihad, which left Mariah wondering whether they should've tried to sneak back to the cabin rather than hiding up at the glen. But, by the same token, she couldn't regret the decision, or what had come after. New memories were precious things.

Not wanting the others to know what had happened between them, she consciously avoided looking at Gray as the helicopter flew them down off the ridge, back to Bear Claw City. Instead, she huddled in the blanket she'd pulled from her knapsack, trying to recapture the warmth of the hot spring without thinking of the things she and Gray had done to each other, the feelings he'd unleashed in her.

It was impossible not to think about the emotions, though. They overwhelmed her, consumed her and made her deeply afraid that she'd done the unthinkable and had once again fallen for the absolute wrong guy.

Realizing that she'd heard someone say her name, she looked to the front of the passenger area of the helicopter, where Gray was huddled with two other agents while talking into a radio headset. He was looking at her, one elegant eyebrow arched to suggest that he'd asked her something. When their eyes met, heat sparked low in her midsection, hotter now than before, because now she knew how it could be with a man like him. Or rather, with *him*.

She cleared her throat. "Sorry, I was zoning out." And then some.

"A car is going to meet us at the landing pad with the statuettes. Once you've pointed out the right one, we'll take it for analysis and the driver will take you to your parents." Gray rapped out the summary, making it clear that what happened next wasn't open to discussion. He wasn't the soldier now, or the man. He was pure, cold federal agent.

"Fine," she said dully, suddenly sick of it all. She'd tried to make the right choices before and she'd been wrong at almost every turn. This time she'd play along with the Feds, and hope for the best. What else could she do? She was tired of fighting when she never actually won.

She must've dozed off after that, because the next thing she knew, the helicopter was landing with a shuddering bump, and she was suddenly surrounded by armed men snapping terse, clipped orders to one another as they hustled her off the aircraft.

Fear kicked in, and she instinctively looked for Gray. He was still talking into his radio headset, but met her eyes and nodded. She couldn't tell if the nod meant "You're okay, go with them and I'll be right behind you," or "It's over."

Knowing they'd said their goodbyes already and it wasn't the time or place to ask for more, if she'd even meant to, she went with her escort. Moments later, she was staring into the trunk of a dark SUV, where her mother's ceramic clowns were arrayed like a small army of terminally cheerful, red-and-white painted gremlins.

"That one," she said, pointing out a floppy-footed guy with green suspenders.

"You're sure?" The question came from Gray's friend, Fairfax, who had hopped out of the SUV as they approached.

"Positive. That's the one Lee kept asking me about when he was holding me prisoner. That's what he wants from me." A stinking clown. There was irony there, she was sure of it. She just couldn't see it through the heartache.

At Fairfax's nod, two of the men guarding her took possession of the statuette, bundling it up and spiriting it away. Fairfax gestured to another man and slammed shut the rear deck of the SUV. When the agent approached, Fairfax gave him low-voiced instructions, then turned to Mariah. "Special Agent Sykes here is going to drive you to your parents'. Do you need anything before you go?" The look in Fairfax's dark blue eyes made the question far less casual than it should have been.

She didn't want to think about what Gray might

have told his friend about them, didn't want the pity she thought she saw in Fairfax's expression. "I'm fine," she said tightly, and yanked open the passenger door of the SUV before either of the men could get it for her. She climbed up and moved to slam the door shut, but Fairfax caught it before she could.

"Gray said he'd call you at the safe house," he said, keeping his voice low so it was just between the two of them.

She shook her head. "He doesn't have to. He doesn't owe me anything."

"He seems to feel differently," Fairfax said. "How about you?"

"I just want to get this over with," she said, which they both knew wasn't an answer.

He seemed to accept it, though. He shut the door, tapped the roof of the SUV and moments later Special Agent Sykes hopped into the driver's seat. Sykes was probably in his late twenties, lean to the point of gauntness, with blond hair and pale eyes that looked almost colorless in the glow of the dashboard displays. He didn't say anything, but that was fine with Mariah. She just wanted to be left alone.

The agent drove them away from the airport, through the city and out the other side, into the 'burbs. A sick feeling gathered in Mariah's stomach as the landmarks started looking all too familiar. "Where is this safe house exactly?"

As he rolled to a stop at a red light, Sykes reached out and patted her hand. "In your case, the word *safe* might be an exaggeration."

Before she fully processed the words, before she could pull away or scream or react at all, he grabbed her wrist, yanked her arm across the console, and plunged a needle into the meat of her forearm.

Mariah screamed and tore away, then grabbed for the door handle. But before she could get the door open, the world began to spin, then yaw. Then go black.

The last thing she was conscious of was Sykes putting both hands back on the steering wheel and hitting the gas when the light went green, his lean-featured face impassive and his voice impossibly gentle when he said, "That's right. I'm taking you home where you belong."

## Chapter Eleven

Gray paced the length of the Bear Claw crime lab, which took up most of the basement of the PD. He was keeping an eye on things inside the lab while Fairfax watched the front and rear entrances, making sure their secure investigation stayed that way.

These days, trust was a hard thing to come by. Gray counted himself lucky that Fax and his fiancée, Chelsea, knew and trusted several members of the Bear Claw PD, who had helped them take down Muhammad Feyd and foil the stadium attack the previous year. Those trusted members of the PD, along with FBI forensic investigator Seth Varitek—also a friend of Chelsea and Fax's—were hunched over the ceramic clown statuette in the main room of the three-room lab, a large area filled with machines and long counters. So far they'd been at it twenty minutes, and hadn't yet figured out what made the clown so important.

"This had better not be a decoy," Gray growled under his breath the next time his pacing brought him near Fairfax.

"If it is, we'll deal," Fax said. "At least it'll free us up to do what we've got to do."

"And what is that?" Gray spun on him. "If this clown thing doesn't pan out and give us a solid lead on where the bastards are and what they're planning next, we're not a damn bit further along than we were before—" He broke off, frustration bringing an unfamiliar tightness to his chest.

"Hey." Fax gripped his shoulder. "She's safe, okay? Sykes called in to say he'd made the delivery, that there were hugs and tears all around when she was reunited with her parents."

Gray stopped dead. "What did you say?"

"Sykes called to say—" A shout from the lab interrupted Fax midsentence.

Brain buzzing with dread, Gray spun on the CSIs. "It's not there anymore, is it?"

Varitek's eyes narrowed. "That's right. We found a space chipped out of the statuette and then concealed again—looks like the size and shape of a flash drive, but it's empty. How did you know?"

"Because Mariah isn't close with her parents, not in the slightest. No tears. No happy reunion." Gray headed for the stairs at a dead run. "Call the safe house. Talk to someone *other* than Sykes and confirm that she's there." But in his gut, he knew she wouldn't be.

Sure enough, by the time he arrived at the in-city safe house, the phone and radio traffic had confirmed that Mariah had never arrived at her intended destination, and Sykes's SUV had been found abandoned in the state park north of the city.

Still, Gray continued on to the safe house. Full of cold rage, he checked in with the security detail and let himself into the second-floor condo where Frank and Ada Shore were being protected.

He didn't know precisely what he'd expected them to look like, based on the few, tight-lipped details Mariah had shared, but he hadn't been prepared for the couple he found holding hands on a love seat in the condo's main room.

Mariah's mother was a small, elegantly dressed woman with short, graying hair and kind eyes. Her father was tall and slightly stooped, with the deflated-balloon look of someone who'd gone through a recent weight loss. His expression, however, went hard when he caught sight of Gray. Letting go of his wife's hands, Frank rose to his full height and faced Gray squarely. "What's happening? Where's Mariah?"

Gray didn't answer immediately because he couldn't trust himself to be civil, and insults weren't going to help him find her. Besides, he wanted to be mindful of the older man's heart condition. Still, he needed answers. "Where would Mawadi take her?" he asked, his voice laced with deadly intent.

Frank's eyes went blank, then heated to fury. "He's got her? What the hell are you people doing? What kind of protection is this? We've given you everything you've asked for, and the one thing we've asked for— that you keep our daughter safe—hasn't happened."

Two years earlier, or maybe even as recently as a couple of weeks before, Gray might have responded with a threat, or by telling Mariah's father exactly what he thought of parents who put themselves first, always. But getting to know Mariah had changed him. She'd reminded him that the victims of terrorism weren't the only ones hurt by the bombs and attacks. The effects reached far and wide, and were sometimes mixed with guilt and culpability, but that didn't make them any less real.

So instead of attacking, he laid it out as simply as he could. "They got past us again. I won't apologize for it because I'm not sorry—I'm furious." He paused, and his voice went rough when he said, "Mawadi already had possession of the computer files he'd hid in the statuette—Sykes took them during transport. So we have to assume that Mawadi took Mariah for revenge. She had the guts to leave him, and for that he wants her dead. More than that, he wants her to suffer—she said that was his way. So I'm asking you—I'm begging you—to think. Where would he take her, someplace nearby, if he wanted her to suffer?"

"I don't…I don't know." Mariah's father seemed to sink into himself, deflating further. "I didn't know any of it. She never told us anything was wrong in her marriage, never even hinted at it."

"That might've had something to do with the fact that you never listened to her," Gray said, unable to help himself. "If you'd—" He snapped off the words. "Never mind. Not my business."

"No, I don't think it is," Ada said. She rose to join her husband, standing at his shoulder to form a united front, one that excluded Gray just as he imagined it had excluded Mariah. But then Ada's expression softened, and she reached out to take one of Gray's hands in both of hers. "But it seems like Mariah thought otherwise."

His voice went thick. "She's told me a few things." And she'd given him a gift beyond measure, he was starting to realize. She'd reminded him how to feel. He'd been numb for so long, he almost couldn't bear all the emotions bombarding him now—fear for her, grief for how he'd left things between them, and anger at the parents who'd made her feel that she had to solve every problem on her own.

"We love her," Ada said simply. "We always have, though we haven't always shown it as we should, and we weren't always the best of parents."

"You took the clown back," he said, which wasn't the most important point by far, but had stuck with him as the crowning injustice. "She defended the damn thing from her bastard of an ex, and you took it away from her."

Ada's eyes filled. "We were moving away. I wanted something that reminded me of her."

"Next time, ask for a damn picture. Or, better yet, stay put and take care of your daughter." Gray knew he was being harsh, and when he saw Frank's color change, going from ruddy to sickly pale, he feared that he'd gone too far, that he'd compromised the older man's health once again in his efforts to do the right thing.

But Frank regained his composure with a visible effort. He gripped his wife's hand as if it were his anchor, and she leaned into him, bumping his arm with her shoulder. The bond between them was palpable;

Gray recognized their true, lifelong love, like the partnership his parents had shared, the connection he'd sought but never found.

Until now, he realized. He'd found that connection with Mariah. It wasn't that they were incompatible, it was more that they were very different on the surface, but alike underneath, in the fundamentals. They were both opinionated and stubborn, comfortable being alone, but so much happier when they were with the right friend—or lover. At least he hoped she felt the same way, because at that moment, he realized that he was so much more alive with her than without her, that he wanted her in his life.

"I'm sorry," Ada said, tears spilling over and tracking down her cheeks. "I don't know where he would take her. We lived less than a half hour away from them, but we barely knew them as a couple."

Gray's head came up. "Wait. Where did they live? Where exactly?"

It had been in the investigative files, but he hadn't done much more than glance at the information in passing, because the small house where the couple had moved right after their marriage had been searched extensively and then released from the evidentiary chain. As far as he knew, it had been sold but never occupied, and still stood empty.

What if that had been part of the plan?

Mariah had gone to her marriage bed a virgin, gone into the marriage full of hopes and dreams, only to see them gradually crushed beneath her husband's insidious brand of evil. What better place to make her suffer and die—in Mawadi's twisted brain, anyway—than back at the house where the torture had truly begun?

Frank thought for a moment, then shook his head. "I'm sorry. I don't know exactly, and my address book is back at home. Somewhere north of the city. I remember that much."

They'd found Sykes's abandoned SUV north of the city.

Gray gritted his teeth. His mother could've recited his last three addresses by heart. At one point, when he'd just wanted to be left alone to wallow, that sort of love had felt smothering. Now he realized that it was a gift.

"Never mind. I'll get my people to look it up." He spun and headed for the door, calling for Fairfax to get on the horn to Johnson and have a team meet them at the address.

"Special Agent Grayson," Ada said from behind him. The soft plea in her voice made him stop, even though every fiber of his being said he had to hurry, that each second could be Mariah's last.

He turned back. "What?"

"Please tell her…please tell her we're sorry."

"Tell her yourself when I bring her out," Gray said. Then he turned away and headed for the car at a dead run, praying that he could get her out, that she and her parents would have a chance for reconciliation. And hoping to hell he got that same chance with her.

MARIAH AWAKENED DISORIENTED, and for a few seconds thought she was still dreaming—a nightmare of times past, when she'd thought she was losing her mind, seeing a demon inside the skin of the man she'd married.

She was back in the bedroom they'd shared, back to awakening with him staring at her, and with the prickly, sore sensation that he'd been fondling her too hard, pinching her breasts to the point of pain, though he'd always denied touching her while she'd slept so deeply she'd been almost certain he'd drugged her.

*Drugged.* The thought brought Sykes's image, and the pain of an injection. The memories snapped her to the present, and warned her that she was in serious trouble. She started to struggle, only to find her wrists and ankles bound tightly and affixed to something solid behind her.

The bastard had tied her to the wall again.

"Awake now, Mrs. Mawadi?" Lee asked, though he hadn't used the name *Mawadi* when they'd been married. They'd been Mr. and Mrs. Chisholm. He nodded and smiled his all-American smile. "Good. I've been waiting for you to come around."

He rose to his feet, making her aware that she wasn't on the bed they'd shared, but rather lying on the carpeted floor of what had once been their bedroom. That was more evidence that she was in the present, that this wasn't a dream. She knew the old house had been stripped of furniture because she'd signed the auction papers herself, though she hadn't been back since the day she'd been escorted out by several FBI agents, including Gray.

*Gray.* The name sighed in her heart, but she didn't

say it aloud, didn't want to give Lee the leverage. Instead, she glared at the man she'd once thought she loved. "Revisiting old haunts, Lee? Not very smart of you. The FBI is keeping watch on this place."

He gave her a backhanded slap, his expression never changing from one of polite indifference. "Don't lie to me. Our information indicates the surveillance was lifted months ago." He smiled, and the look in his eyes chilled her blood. "You and I should have a little while longer before the feebs track us down. Plenty of time to get reacquainted."

Mariah tasted blood and her own fear. Her insides trembled and she was sorely tempted to crawl inside herself and pretend none of this was happening. But she wasn't that woman anymore. She was tougher, stronger. So rather than let loose the whimper that wanted to break free, she said, "What did you hide inside the statue, Lee? What didn't you want them to find?"

His face split in a self-congratulatory smile and he drew back, fiddling with a small, flat remote control–like box, tossing it from one hand to the other. "Nothing that'll help you, that's for sure. Those files are part of the larger plan, one we've been working on since well before I picked you up at that crummy coffee bar. And the clown…ah, the clown. It was pretty freaking clever of me, wouldn't you say? I figured if you died, your cold bitch of a mother would take it back. If you lived, I figured you'd keep the stupid thing, even if you ditched the rest of our stuff. Which I knew you'd do, because you're just what al-Jihad said you'd be—a disloyal bitch who ran the second things got tough."

"You tried to kill me. You call that things getting tough?"

He hit her again, then sucked her blood from his knuckles. "You don't leave a man like me, Mariah. I don't believe in divorce. I don't recognize the court's power to do something like that. Which means you're not only still married to me, you're an adulterer."

"How did you know—" She bit off the words, but it was too late.

"I didn't before, but I do now. You just confirmed it, my unfaithful little wife." He leaned in and put his face very close to hers, eyes suddenly blazing. "It was Grayson, wasn't it? I heard about the way the two of you were looking at each other."

The way he said it made it seem as though al-Jihad had people throughout the local and federal arms of the investigation. Mariah knew Gray suspected there were insiders, but didn't think he had any idea of the extent. If she could just get to him…

Who was she kidding? She didn't want to see him to pass along information on al-Jihad's resources and plans, or not really. She wanted to see *him,* to be with him. She wanted to talk to him, to convince him that they weren't so different after all. They clicked. They fit. They made sense.

And she loved him. When she came right down to it, that was the truth in her soul, the emotion she'd been avoiding for too long.

She'd been thinking of herself as a fighter, but she hadn't fought for what mattered most—her future.

Lee smacked her again, this time on the other cheek.

"Answer me, bitch! Tell me you spread your legs for some loser FBI agent whose own boss doesn't even trust him not to screw up." He got very close, practically screaming the words into her face. "Tell me!"

"Yes," she said very clearly, speaking through a face gone numb and sore. "I was with Grayson. I love him."

"And the feeling's mutual," Gray's voice said, snapping Mariah's attention to the bedroom doorway. He stood there, coldly furious, his attention fixed on Lee, though she knew he was as acutely aware of her as she was of him.

"Gray." She sighed his name on a whisper of hope and a whole lot of fear, because she'd also seen the flash in Lee's eyes. Not fear, but triumph. He'd planned for this, maybe even intended it. *Lee, don't,* she wanted to say, but didn't because she knew her pleas would only add to his pleasure.

"FBI. Hands up and get the hell away from her," Gray growled, entering the room with his weapon drawn. Other men, including Fairfax, were crowded into the hallway behind him. "We've got the house surrounded."

"Oh, I'll raise my hands, all right." Lee eased away from Mariah, then held up his hands to show the object he'd been fiddling with since Mariah awakened.

It was a small technical-looking box with a couple of buttons and a digital display. He held a yellow toggle with his thumb, and the digital countdown showed less than seven minutes remaining.

Mariah was no expert, but based on what she little she knew, and the way Gray and the others froze, she had to assume it was a detonator of some sort.

Lee's tone was gloating when he said, "The basement of this place is loaded with explosives. You shoot me and I let go of this trigger, this place goes up immediately. You play along, and you've got three minutes and change to get your girlfriend out of here."

"Define *play along*," Gray said tightly.

"First off, get your agent friends out of here. This is between the two of us."

"Clear the building and push the perimeter back," Gray snapped without looking behind him. There was a mad scramble of bodies. All but one. "You too, Fax," he growled. "Get out of here. For Chelsea's sake, if nothing else."

Fairfax hesitated, then turned and left.

When the three of them were alone, Gray said, "Now what? You know you're not getting out of here alive. We've got the perimeter completely locked up."

"Maybe I don't want to get out." Lee stood and backed across the room, toward the closet he'd used for his clothes and forbidden her from entering when they'd lived there. "Maybe there's something I want to show you, instead."

"Freeze!" Gray barked. "Stop moving right now, or—"

Lee tossed the detonator at him. The trigger snapped open, but instead of an explosion, it brought a gout of choking gray smoke spewing from the handheld unit. Under the cover of that smoke, Lee bolted for the closet, yanking open the door, then stooping to pull up a trapdoor that Mariah hadn't ever seen before.

Shouting for the other agents to get their butts back

into the house, Gray fired several rounds into the smoke. Under that cover he lunged forward, grabbing for Lee. He made contact, getting Lee around the waist and throwing him to the ground, but lost hold of his weapon, which went skittering across the floor.

Choking and gagging on the smoke, her eyes watering profusely, Mariah could only lie helpless and watch as the men grappled and struggled. Gray landed two good punches, but then Lee drove his elbow into Gray's temple.

Gray reeled back, dazed. Lee ripped away and leaped into the closet, disappearing down the dark opening revealed beneath the trapdoor.

"Get in here!" Gray bellowed. When Fax appeared at a dead run, Gray waved to the opening. "Down there. Careful, but make it fast. We've got a few minutes to get out of range, assuming the bastard didn't lie about the explosives."

"He didn't," Fax said quietly. "The outside team's fiber optics located them in the basement. And you were right, this was a distraction, too. There's been a riot at the Supermax. The warden's dead, along with two cops. One was the IA detective, Romo Sampson."

"Damn." Gray shook his head. "We can't help them now, though. Get moving."

As Fax palmed his flashlight and dropped through the trapdoor, Gray grabbed his weapon, scooped up the smoke bomb and lobbed it out into the hallway. Then he crouched down beside Mariah and started yanking at her bonds.

Her tears welled up and spilled over. "He's getting away."

"Yes, he is." But although Gray's voice was matter-of-fact, it wasn't the slightest bit cool. In fact, it trembled slightly.

"Go," she urged. "Remember how you said—"

"I remember most of what I've said to you," he interrupted, "and I'm not proud of all of it. Some of it was downright stupid, some of it dead wrong. But what I said just now? That's the truth. It's what matters." He pressed his forehead to hers. "I love you. I'm sorry it took me so long to see that and to say it. You're my priority, you're what matters most. There'll be another chance for us to get Mawadi and al-Jihad. If I leave you here, there won't be another chance for me to save myself and take my life in a new direction."

As he said that, her shackles came undone and she was free.

Sobbing, she threw her arms around his neck. "I love you. Oh, God. I was so afraid you wouldn't come."

"You won't ever have to worry about that again, because I'll always be right there beside you, from now on." His words were muffled against her as he held her close and lifted her, and they turned for the door. Gray raised his voice. "Time to go, Fairfax."

Fax's voice floated up. "There's a tunnel headed north. I'm going to—"

"You're going to get your ass back up here or I'll tell Chelsea on you," Gray said calmly.

There was a brief pause, then Fairfax reappeared, pulling himself out of the hidden tunnel.

Without a word, the men ushered Mariah outside, to a car parked well beyond the blast zone. There was a brief discussion about disarming the bomb, but it was deemed too late. Instead, the other members of the armed response agents hustled to clear the nearby buildings.

As the seconds ticked down, Mariah looked toward the house she'd entered with wonderful dreams and left in the grip of a nightmare.

Gray slipped an arm around her waist. "Let's go."

"No." She shook her head. "I want to see it. Are we far enough back?"

"Yeah."

They were standing there, partially sheltered behind one of the dark SUVs, when there was a *whump* of detonation, a shudder in the ground beneath their feet…and then her house seemed to sag and settle in on itself. The roof tilted, the walls bowed out and everything slid off to one side. Moments later, flames licked from one of the lower windows.

Mariah thought that, in an odd way, it was both anticlimactic and cathartic.

In the distance, a fire engine's siren began to wail. Mariah, though, couldn't find any tears. She couldn't find any joy, either. She was, quite simply, numb. So much had happened so quickly that she couldn't begin to process it.

"He said the hidden files had something to do with al-Jihad's grand strategy, something he'd been planning since long before Lee and I met. I think…I think he meant that marrying me wasn't just about the malls. He made it seem like there was more, that the bombs, and maybe even the jail time, was all part of something bigger, a plan they haven't put into motion yet."

"That plays," Gray agrees. "We'll have you give a full report, go over everything he said or did." He tightened his arm and looked down at her. "I'll be there, and I promise—no browbeating this time around."

Incredibly, she felt a bubble of laughter lodge in her throat. "I think I'm tough enough to hold my own now. Bring on the rubber hoses, Mr. FBI guy."

"Yeah, you're strong enough to make it on your own now." He leaned down and dropped a kiss on her lips. "But you're not going to have to. And neither am I."

And as she closed her eyes and opened herself up to his kiss, and the future that had begun to unreel in front of her, she knew he was absolutely right. Each of them was strong enough to cope with whatever came next, as Bear Claw City dealt with the fallout of the fatal prison riots. But the lovely thing was, she and Gray wouldn't have to handle it alone, not anymore.

They'd deal with everything together.

\* \* \* \* \*

*Don't miss*
*Jessica Andersen's*
*next BEAR CLAW CREEK CRIME LAB book,*
*INTERNAL AFFAIRS.*
*On sale in October 2009,*
*only from Harlequin Intrigue!*

*Celebrate 60 years of pure reading pleasure with Harlequin!*

To commemorate the event, Harlequin Intrigue®
is thrilled to invite you to the wedding of
The Colby Agency's J. T. Baxley and his bride,
Eve Mattson.

That is, of course, if J.T. can find the woman who
left him at the altar. Considering he's a private
investigator for one of the top agencies in the
country—the best of the best—that shouldn't be
a problem. The real setback is that his bride isn't
who she appears to be…and her mysterious past
has put them both in danger.

*Enjoy an exclusive glimpse of Debra Webb's latest
addition to*
### THE COLBY AGENCY:
### ELITE RECONNAISSANCE DIVISION

*THE BRIDE'S SECRETS*

*Available August 2009 from Harlequin Intrigue®*

The dark figures on the dock were still firing. The bullets cutting through the surface of the water without the warning boom of shots told Eve they were using silencers.

That was to her benefit. Silencers decreased the accuracy of every shot and lessened the range.

She grabbed for the rocks. Scrambled through the darkness. Bumped her knee on a boulder. Cursed.

Burrowing into the waist-deep grass, she kept low and crawled forward. Faster. Pushed harder. Needed as much distance as possible.

Shots pinged on the rocks.

J.T. scrambled alongside her.

He was breathing hard.

They had to stay close to the ground until they reached the next row of warehouses. Even though she was relatively certain they were out of range at this point, she wasn't taking any risks. And she wasn't slowing down.

J.T. had to keep up.

The splat of a bullet hitting the ground next to Eve had her rolling left. Maybe they weren't completely out of range.

She bumped J.T. He grunted.

His injured arm. Dammit. She could apologize later.

Half a dozen more yards.

Almost in the clear.

As she reached the cover of the alley between the first two warehouses she tensed.

Silence.

No pings or splats.

She glanced back at the dock. Deserted.

Time to run.

Her car was parked another block down.

Pushing to her feet, she sprinted forward. The wet bag dragged at her shoulder. She ignored it.

By the time she reached the lot where her car was parked, she had dug the keys from her pocket and hit the fob. Six seconds later she was behind the wheel. She hit the ignition as J.T. collapsed into the passenger seat. Tires squealed as she spun out of the slot.

"What the hell did you do to me?"

From the corner of her eye she watched him shake his head in an attempt to clear it.

He would be pissed when she told him about the tranquilizer.

She'd needed him cooperative until she formulated a plan. A drug-induced state of unconsciousness had been the fastest and most efficient method to ensure his continued solidarity.

"I can't really talk right now." Eve weaved into the

right lane as the street widened to four lanes. What she needed was traffic. It was Saturday night—shouldn't be that difficult to find as soon as they were out of the old warehouse district.

A glance in the rearview mirror warned that their unwanted company had caught up.

Sensing her tension, J.T. turned to peer over his left shoulder.

"I hope you have a plan B."

She shot him a look. "There's always plan G." Then she pulled the Glock out of her waistband.

Cutting the steering wheel left, she slid between two vehicles. Another veer to the right and she'd put several cars between hers and the enemy.

She was betting they wouldn't pull out the firepower in the open like this, but a girl could never be too sure when it came to an unknown enemy.

Deep blending was the way to go.

Two traffic lights ahead the marquis of a movie theater provided exactly the opportunity she was looking for.

The digital numbers on the dash indicated it was just past midnight. Perfect timing. The late movie would be purging its audience into the crowd of teen-agers who liked hanging out in the parking lot.

She took a hard right onto the property that sported a twelve-screen theater, numerous fast-food hot spots and a chain superstore. Speeding across the lot, she selected a lane of parking slots. Pulling in as close to the theater entrance as possible, she shut off the engine and reached for her door.

"Let's go."

Thankfully, he didn't argue.

Rounding the hood of her car, she shoved the Glock into her bag, then wrapped her arm around J.T.'s and merged into the crowd.

With her free hand she finger-combed her long hair. It was soaked, as were her clothes. The kids she bumped into noticed, gave her death-ray glares.

They just didn't know.

As she and J.T. moved in closer to the building, she grabbed a baseball cap from an innocent bystander. The crowd made it easy. The kid who owned the cap had made it even easier by stuffing the cap bill-first into his waistband at the small of his back.

Pushing through the loitering crowd, she made her way to the side of the building next to the main entrance. She pushed J.T. against the wall and dropped her bag to the ground. Peeled off her tee and let it fall.

His gaze instantly zeroed in on her breasts, where the cami she wore had glued to her skin like an extra layer. A zing of desire shot through her veins.

Not the time.

With a flick of her wrist she twisted her hair up and clamped the cap atop the blonde mass.

"They're coming," J.T. muttered as he gazed at some point beyond her.

"Yeah, I know." She planted her palms against the wall on either side of him and leaned in. "Keep your eyes open. Let me know when they're inside."

Then she planted her lips on his.

* * * * *

*Will J.T. and Eve be caught in the moment?*
*Or will Eve get the chance to reveal*
*all of her secrets?*
*Find out in*
*THE BRIDE'S SECRETS*
*by Debra Webb*
*Available August 2009 from Harlequin Intrigue*®

From *New York Times* bestselling authors

# CARLA NEGGERS

## SUSAN MALLERY
## KAREN HARPER

More Than Words:
STORIES OF
STRENGTH

They're your neighbors, your aunts, your sisters and your best friends. They're women across North America committed to changing and enriching lives, one good deed at a time. Three of these exceptional women have been selected as recipients of Harlequin's More Than Words award. And three *New York Times* bestselling authors have kindly offered their creativity to write original short stories inspired by these real-life heroines.

Visit **www.HarlequinMoreThanWords.com**
to find out more, or to nominate
a real-life heroine in your life.

**Proceeds from the sale of this book will be
reinvested in Harlequin's charitable initiatives.**

*Available in March 2009 wherever books are sold.*

# You're invited to join our Tell Harlequin Reader Panel!

By joining our new reader panel you will:

- Receive Harlequin® books—they are FREE and yours to keep with no obligation to purchase anything!
- Participate in fun online surveys
- Exchange opinions and ideas with women just like you
- Have a say in our new book ideas and help us publish the best in women's fiction

*In addition, you will have a chance to win great prizes and receive special gifts! See Web site for details. Some conditions apply. Space is limited.*

To join, visit us at

## www.TellHarlequin.com.

# REQUEST YOUR FREE BOOKS!

## 2 FREE NOVELS
## PLUS 2
## FREE GIFTS!

◆ HARLEQUIN®

# INTRIGUE®

## Breathtaking Romantic Suspense

**YES!** Please send me 2 FREE Harlequin Intrigue® novels and my 2 FREE gifts (gifts are worth about $10). After receiving them, if I don't wish to receive any more books, I can return the shipping statement marked "cancel." If I don't cancel, I will receive 6 brand-new novels every month and be billed just $4.24 per book in the U.S. or $4.99 per book in Canada. That's a savings of close to 15% off the cover price! It's quite a bargain! Shipping and handling is just 50¢ per book.* I understand that accepting the 2 free books and gifts places me under no obligation to buy anything. I can always return a shipment and cancel at any time. Even if I never buy another book from Harlequin, the two free books and gifts are mine to keep forever.

182 HDN EYTR  382 HDN EYT3

| | |
|---|---|
| Name | (PLEASE PRINT) |
| Address | Apt. # |
| City | State/Prov. | Zip/Postal Code |

Signature (if under 18, a parent or guardian must sign)

Mail to the **Harlequin Reader Service**:
**IN U.S.A.:** P.O. Box 1867, Buffalo, NY 14240-1867
**IN CANADA:** P.O. Box 609, Fort Erie, Ontario L2A 5X3

Not valid to current subscribers of Harlequin Intrigue books.

**Are you a current subscriber of Harlequin Intrigue books
and want to receive the larger-print edition?
Call 1-800-873-8635 today!**

* Terms and prices subject to change without notice. Prices do not include applicable taxes. Sales tax applicable in N.Y. Canadian residents will be charged applicable provincial taxes and GST. Offer not valid in Quebec. This offer is limited to one order per household. All orders subject to approval. Credit or debit balances in a customer's account(s) may be offset by any other outstanding balance owed by or to the customer. Please allow 4 to 6 weeks for delivery. Offer available while quantities last.

**Your Privacy:** Harlequin is committed to protecting your privacy. Our Privacy Policy is available online at www.eHarlequin.com or upon request from the Reader Service. From time to time we make our lists of customers available to reputable third parties who may have a product or service of interest to you. If you would prefer we not share your name and address, please check here. ☐

HI09R

**Stay up-to-date on all your romance reading news!**

The Harlequin Inside Romance newsletter is a **FREE** quarterly newsletter highlighting our upcoming series releases and promotions!

**Go to**
**eHarlequin.com/InsideRomance**
**or e-mail us at**
**InsideRomance@Harlequin.com**
**to sign up to receive**
**your FREE newsletter today!**

---

You can also subscribe by writing to us at: HARLEQUIN BOOKS
Attention: Customer Service Department
P.O. Box 9057, Buffalo, NY 14269-9057

*Please allow 4-6 weeks for delivery of the first issue by mail.*

IRNBPAQ209

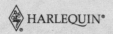 HARLEQUIN®

# INTRIGUE®

## COMING NEXT MONTH

### Available August 11, 2009

#### #1149 STEALING THUNDER by Patricia Rosemoor
*The McKenna Legacy*
Fearing his love is a curse, the charming cowboy avoids relationships—until he meets the one woman he can't live without. Now someone is threatening her life, and there is nothing he wouldn't do to protect her.

#### #1150 MORE THAN A MAN by Rebecca York
*43 Light Street*
His bride knows that her protective billionaire is no ordinary man, but she doesn't know all of his secrets. Can he trust her with the truth and shield her from his enemies?

#### #1151 THE BRIDE'S SECRETS by Debra Webb
*Colby Agency: Elite Reconnaissance Division*
A Colby Agency P.I. discovers that there is more to the woman he meant to marry than meets the eye, and he won't rest until he knows whether their relationship was a lie. But first he must find his runaway bride.

#### #1152 COWBOY TO THE CORE by Joanna Wayne
*Special Ops Texas*
He spent years serving his country in a special ops unit, but now this military man longs to return to his cowboy ways. Back home in Texas, his dreams of the quiet life are shattered when he meets a woman in danger…a woman who rouses all his protective instincts.

#### #1153 FAMILIAR SHOWDOWN by Caroline Burnes
*Fear Familiar*
Betrayed by her presumed dead—and double agent—fiancé, the ranch manager won't let another man lie to her. Now she learns that her new hire is really an undercover agent, and he's looking for the truth. Well, so is she! Will he be the last straw or her salvation?

#### #1154 NAVAJO COURAGE by Aimée Thurlo
*Brotherhood of Warriors*
To catch a serial killer, her department brings in a Navajo investigator. Although she may not agree with his methods, she can't ignore his unique skills or his sensuous touch. But the killer may be closer than they think….

www.eHarlequin.com

HICNMBPA0709